# The
# Island of
# Lost Horses

## Stacy Gregg

### HarperCollins *Children's Books*

First published in hardback in Great Britain by
HarperCollins *Children's Books* in 2014.
This edition published in 2015.
HarperCollins *Children's Books* is a division of HarperCollins*Publishers* Ltd,
1 London Bridge Street
London SE1 9GF

The HarperCollins *Children's Books* website address is
www.harpercollins.co.uk

For Stacy's blog, competitions, interviews and more, visit
www.stacygregg.co.uk

1

ISBN 978-0-00-758027-9

Printed and bound in England by Clays Ltd, St Ives plc

FSC                                                                    promote
the re                                                                 rying the
FSC l                                                                  hey come
f                                                                      and

Find out more about HarperCollins and the environment at
**www.harpercollins.co.uk/green**

Photograph © Carolyn Haslett

*S*tacy Gregg is the author of eighteen books including *The Princess and the Foal*, winner of the Children's Choice Junior Fiction award at the New Zealand Post Book Awards for Children and Young Adults, and has reinvigorated the pony genre with her popular series *Pony Club Secrets* and *Pony Club Rivals*.

*The Island of Lost Horses* is based on the extraordinary true story of the Abaco Barb horse, a mystery that has remained unsolved for over five hundred years.

# The Diary of Beatriz Ortega

## 12th April, 2014

I am writing this as fast as I can. The doors on the *Phaedra* don't lock, and Mom could walk in any moment. I have no privacy. I am the only twelve-year-old girl I know who has to share a room with her mom. I have pointed out how unfair it is, the way the jellyfish equipment takes up the whole front of the boat, but Mom won't listen. Typical – the jellyfish get their own room and I don't.

I'm not trying to make excuses for my handwriting or anything, but if it is all scrawly that's because my arm's so trembly I can hardly hold the pen. I think it's from gripping on to the tractor for so long. The entire way home I had to cling to the wheel arch, sitting up there behind Annie like a parrot perched on a pirate's shoulder. The way she drove along those rutted jungle tracks, I was petrified I was going to lose hold and fall beneath the wheels.

By the time we reached the bay and I could see the *Phaedra*, my body had been shaken up like a can of fizzy drink.

There was no sign of Mom as the tractor lumbered over the dunes and down the beach towards the sea. I was kind of relieved, to tell the truth. The whole time at Annie's house I had been desperate to get back to the boat, but now that I was home I felt sick at the thought of facing Mom. She would be furious with me. I had been gone for two whole days...

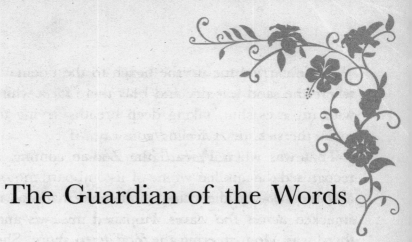

# The Guardian of the Words

Annie jolted to a stop and I lost my grip on the wheel arch and fell to the sand, collapsing like jelly out of a mould, my legs giving way beneath me.

"Bee-a-trizz!" Annie leapt down from the tractor and hooked her arms under my armpits to lift me to my feet again.

"For heaven's sake, child!"

She was really strong for a little old lady. She held me like a rag doll, so that my feet dragged through the sand and my face was buried against her chest. I could smell the cotton of her dress and see where the blue floral pattern had gone all yellowed with sweat.

9

Annie carried me up the beach to the tidemark where the sand was dry and I lay there for a while with my eyes shut, taking deep breaths, trying to make the sick, dizzy feeling go away.

That was when I heard the Zodiac coming. I recognised the familiar whine of its outboard motor and the *slap-slap* the rubber inflatable made as it smacked across the waves. I opened my eyes and there was Mom steering the Zodiac to shore. She gestured frantically to me and I gave her a feeble wave in return. I felt like I was going to throw up.

"Wait here, Bee-a-trizz." Annie headed down to the water to help bring the Zodiac in. She stood knee-deep in the waves, holding it steady, and Mom jumped out and left her there as she ran up the beach to me.

"Beatriz!" She dropped to her knees beside me. "Oh my God, Bee!"

"Hi, Mom," I managed a weak smile. When she touched my face her hand felt like ice against my skin.

"Beatriz, you're burning up!"

"I'm OK," I insisted. "I just got a little sunburnt."

"OK?" Mom looked horrified. "We have to get you to a hospital…"

"No." I pushed myself up off the sand. The world was spinning around me. "I'm fine. Honest…"

"De child be al'right."

It was Annie.

"I'm sorry?" Mom said, clearly shocked at the declaration from this stranger. "Are you a doctor?"

"Bee-a-trizz don' be wantin' no doctors," Annie replied. "Child had de fever real bad, so I keep her to sleep at ma crib til day-clean. De fever broke, so she be al'right now…"

"At your place? She's been missing for two days…" Mom's voice was tense. *Here we go*, I thought. Mom was going to grill Annie until she got the whole story. She was going to hear all about the horse and the mud flats and Annie finding me…

But Annie's attention had been caught by the *Phaedra*, moored about forty metres offshore. She gave a flick of her head, gesturing at the boat with her lips, using them the same way other people used their hands to point at stuff.

"You all alone on dat tink?"

Mom's eyes flitted briefly to the boat, then back to Annie. I could see that she was suddenly aware that we were in the middle of nowhere with no one else around except this weird old lady with her tractor.

"Yes," Mom said warily. "I mean, alone with Beatriz – the two of us."

Annie frowned. "You takin' a vacation?"

My mom shook her head. "I'm a marine biologist. I'm working on a research paper for Florida University, studying the migratory patterns of sea thimble jellyfish…"

Annie grunted. She had lost interest and began to walk back to her tractor.

"Wait!" Mom said. "I mean… Thank you. For bringing Beatriz back. I have been worried sick…"

"De child be al'right. No need for worryin'," Annie said. She clambered back up on to the tractor seat, yanking at her skirt to get comfortable. Then she turned the key in the ignition and stuck her bare foot down hard on the tractor pedal. The rattle and burr of the engine instantly killed any hopes Mom might have had for further conversation.

Annie shoved her straw hat down hard on her dreadlocks. "De island be a dangerous place," she said. She was gazing over at the dunes where we had come from, taking in the far distant end of the island where the mud flats lay. "Very dangerous. You best be careful…"

Then, the tractor rumbled forward and Annie

swung the steering wheel, turning the tractor so close to me, I thought she might run over my toes with those giant tyres. Then she raised her hand to flick me a goodbye wave and set off, the tyres digging zigzag patterns into the smooth white sand.

Annie's battered straw hat was the last thing I saw as she crested the dunes and sank out of sight.

"That woman is flat-out crazy."

My mom, making her usual proclamations.

"Annie's not crazy," I countered. "She's my friend…" Although that really wasn't true, was it? Annie gave me the creeps. The whole time I had been at her place I had wanted to leave. But I would never admit that to Mom.

"You stayed at her house?" Mom launched into it. "What were you thinking? Why didn't you call me?"

I pulled my phone out of my pocket. It was sandy and crusted with salt, its insides totally soaked.

"It died," I said. And the thought briefly flashed into my mind, should I tell Mom what had happened to me? *No.* I stopped myself.

*If she knows what happened then she won't let you go back there — and you must go back. You have to see your horse again…*

"Mom?" I took a deep breath. "Can we go back to the boat, please? I think I'm going to throw up…"

I managed to control the nausea, even with the Zodiac bouncing and skittering across the waves. I sat in the prow on the bench seat, focusing hard on the horizon, which is what you do to stop feeling seasick.

When we reached the *Phaedra*, Mom tied off the inflatable while I dragged myself up the ladder and on to the deck. I was still a bit shaky and I stumbled and fell forward, grabbing the side of the boat to stay upright.

"Are you sure you don't need a doctor?" Mom asked. It was a silly question. Even if I did need a doctor where would we find one in a wilderness reserve on the outer edge of the Bahamas?

"I just need to lie down," I insisted.

"Do you want me to make you something to eat?" Mom offered.

I shook my head gently. "No thanks, Mom. I just need to sleep."

I made my way past the steering cabin and the kitchen on the upper deck, gripping the railings the whole way, and then down the narrow stairs that led to our room.

Below deck there are two rooms. The room at the front of the boat is where the jellyfish tanks and monitors and equipment are kept. And the other room is for me and Mom. On my side the walls are covered with horse pictures. The best one is of Meredith Michaels-Beerbaum jumping her horse Shutterfly over this huge water jump at the Olympics.

I flopped down face first on my bunk mattress, my sunburn throbbing, body aching. Then I thought about the diary and I forced myself to sit up again.

I had dumped my backpack on the floor and I reached out and grasped it, dragging it closer so I could unzip it. The ancient diary was right at the top where I had packed it, bound up in filthy, grey cloth.

I noticed as I unwrapped it that the rags were trimmed with tattered lace and there was even a collar with a buttonhole. I guessed the cloth had once been an old-fashioned shirt, but it was so decayed it was hard to imagine anyone ever wearing it.

I put the cloth aside and held the diary in my hands, my fingers tracing the stiff cracks in the leather, the letters stamped on the front.

I was about to open it to the page where I had

last finished reading when there were footsteps on the stairs.

"Bee?" I hurriedly wrapped the diary in its cloth and shoved it back inside the backpack. My heart was pounding. I waited a beat, expecting the door to open.

"Yeah?"

"I'm going to cook some pasta. You want some?"

"Uhh," I hesitated, "no thanks, Mom. I'm not hungry."

"OK."

I waited for a heartbeat or two and then I heard her go back up the stairs. I was about to reach over and take the ancient diary out of the backpack again when a thought occurred to me.

I got up from my bunk and pulled open the drawer underneath where my books were kept. I had to dig through the pile, and for a moment I thought maybe it wasn't even there. But here it was, right at the very bottom. It was smaller than I remembered it, with a blue cover and pale yellow lined pages. I opened my 'Year 5' diary and was relieved to find that, as I remembered, most of it was blank.

My handwriting hadn't changed much over the past three years since I wrote these entries.

The diary had been a school assignment and our teacher Mrs Moskowitz graded it. We were supposed to write our feelings but I never did. Even though Mom and Dad were fighting. This was just before they broke up, before we left Florida.

I didn't mention anything about horses either. I was worried that someone might grab the diary off me in class and read it out loud and I already got teased about being a 'horsey girl'.

Most of the entries were about what I ate for lunch and who I sat next to in class and stuff. On the last page I had written all about how Kristen Adams and I were the bestest friends in the whole of Year 5. I winced a bit when I read that. Some BFF. She hadn't returned my emails for at least two years.

Anyway, once I'd read that page I ripped them all out – the ones with writing on them. I tore them carefully so as not to disturb the blank pages and I balled up the used ones and tossed them aside on my bed. Then I propped myself up on my pillows and smoothed down the first clear page. It felt good to have that empty page looking back at me – waiting for me to put something on it.

I thought back to when Annie had given me

Felipa's diary. She had acted really serious about it, handing it to me like it was a big deal. "Bee-a-trizz," she said. "You be de guardian of de words now."

At the time I thought she meant that because Felipa's diary was written in Spanish and so I could understand it, I should look after it. But now I realised that maybe Annie meant something more than that. She said I was the *guardian of the words*. So maybe my own words mattered too? After everything that had happened to me over the past two days, out on the mud flats and at Annie's house, I finally had something important to write. I had my own story to tell.

It wouldn't be like the old pages that I had torn away. It would be true this time, like diaries are meant to be, but it would be amazing too. And it would begin with the day that I found my horse. Running wild in the most impossible place you could imagine. Here, on this tiny island, a million miles from anywhere, on the outer edge of the Caribbean.

# Great Abaco

If things are going to make any sense at all then I need to backtrack a little and explain how I came to be on Great Abaco Island.

Mom and I had arrived, like we always do, in the wake of a bloom. A bloom is the name for a herd of jellyfish. That is what Mom does – she tracks jellyfish and studies their breeding patterns.

I was nine years old when Mom yanked me out of school and straight into the middle of nowhere. She's been dragging me around on the *Phaedra* with her for three years now, back and forth around the islands so that a map of the Bahamas has been seared into my brain.

Jellyfish, by the way, are totally brainless. I'm not

being mean just because they are taking up what should be my bedroom – it's the truth. Mom says they cope perfectly well without a brain. She says that Nature, unlike people, is non-judgemental about such matters. But I think Nature needs to take a good hard look at itself because it has invented some really stupid stuff. Did you know that a jellyfish's mouth and bottom is the same hole? Eughh!

Even without brains, jellies can get together and bloom, and when they do we follow them. Our boat, the *Phaedra*, is real pretty. She's painted all white with her name written in swirly blue letters above the waterline so that it seems to dance on the waves.

The *Phaedra* was designed as a lobster trawler, so she can only do 12 knots an hour. Which is OK since the jellyfish blooms that we chase never move faster than two knots.

Some of the islands that the jellies lead us to are really small, not much more than a reef and a few trees. Others are huge with big hotels and water parks, and at Christmas time when the tourists come they turn into Disneylands.

This was the very first time we had been to Great Abaco. It's a remote jungle island, a long way from the mainland of Nassau, and we had charted our course to arrive at the island's marina at Marsh Harbour so we could take a mooring for the night and buy supplies and refuel.

That first evening, instead of cooking onboard in our tiny kitchen, we went ashore and Mom treated us to dinner at Wally's. It's the local scuba divers' hangout: a bright pink two-storey place, run-down but in a nice way. We sat on the balcony and I had a conch burger, which I always order, and fries and key lime pie. I was halfway through my dessert, when I asked Mom about moving back to Florida.

The funny thing is, when we left Florida Mom had me totally convinced about how much fun our lives would be. It would be an adventure. I'd be skipping out on school and travelling the high seas – like a pirate or something.

Trust me – it is not like that at all.

For starters, I still do school. Only now I am a creepy home-schooler. I do correspondence classes and workbooks and talk to my tutors over the internet.

"I have no friends here," I told Mom as I ate my pie.

When I left school everyone made this huge fuss about how much they would miss me and stay in touch. Especially Kristen, making a big show of how we would be Best Friends Forever. Forever, it turns out, was a couple of months and then the emails and Skype just stopped.

"Well maybe you need to make more of an effort," Mom countered.

This was what she always said. But she couldn't say it was my fault about the horses.

In Florida we had a stables just down the road. I would park up my bike there after school on the way home and feed the horses over the fence. I had been begging Mom for lessons since I was really little and right before we left she had promised I could start.

"You did," I said. "You promised."

Mom sighed. "Sometimes things don't work out the way we want…"

The thing is I have this whole plan where I become an amazing rider and go to the Olympics. Mom knows this because it is all I talk about.

"I am running out of time," I told her. "Meredith Michaels-Beerbaum had already won her first Grand Prix by the time she was my age. How am I supposed to train for the Olympics when I'm stuck on a boat?"

Mom reached over with her spoon and helped herself to a chunk out of my key lime pie.

"Why don't you train for the swim team instead?" she offered.

"Mom! You're not taking me seriously," I said. "I want to go back to Florida."

"No."

"You can't just say no. I am a US citizen and I have rights."

"You have the right to remain silent," my mother said.

"How about if I lived with Dad? I could visit you in the school holidays…"

"Beatriz!" I cannot even mention Dad without her getting mad. "I have told you to drop it, OK? That's not an option. You live with me. End of discussion."

*** 

The following morning we set off at dawn, chugging out of the marina and heading South along the shoreline of Cherokee Sound where the tangerine, mint and lemon-sherbet-coloured beach cottages dotted the shore. By the time we reached the end of the Sound, the cottages with their bright colours and pretty gardens had disappeared and the coastline had become colourless and windswept. The white sand beaches were deserted, and instead of manicured flowerbeds there were nothing but tangles of sea grape, mangroves and cabbage trees.

This was the Great Abaco wilderness reserve. The whole southernmost end of the island was uninhabited, cloaked in jungles of Caribbean pine, snakewood and pigeon berry. From the bow of the boat the jungle seemed to sit like a black cloud across the land as we moved by.

"We're going to anchor here." Mom throttled back the engine.

"Where is here?" I asked, peering out suspiciously at the desolate shoreline.

Mom kept her eyes down on the scanner as she steered the *Phaedra*.

"Shipwreck Bay," she said.

She handed me the map, her eyes still glued to the scanner and I could see now why she was steering so carefully. There was a hidden reef at the entrance to the bay, so close to the surface that it was almost impossible to navigate your way through.

I went to the side of the *Phaedra* and stared down into the water. It kept changing colour as we passed over the reef, turning dark indigo where the water was deepest. I could see shadows moving beneath the waves. Reef sharks, big ones by the look of it. And then another shadow, deeper down below, which looked like the outline of a ship. I lay down on the deck of the *Phaedra* and hung my head over the side so that I could get a better look, staring down into the dark water. It was a ship all right. As we motored over it I could make out the shape of the mast.

"Bee?" Mom called out to me. "Go drop the anchor for me, will you?"

Mom kept the engines of the *Phaedra* running as she turned into the wind and I ran downstairs, going through our room and into the jellyfish quarters to engage the anchor winch. I pressed down hard on the button and the motor began to grind, unravelling the chain link and lowering the anchor into the sea. I watched it unravel until the marker hit twelve metres and stopped. The anchor had struck the seabed.

By the time I got back up on deck Mom had already started work. She had her laptop out and various sea charts were spread over the kitchen table.

"What are you doing today, Bee?" she asked me.

Sometimes when Mom is working, I stay onboard and lie on the deck and read books. I am brown as a berry from all that reading. Mom says it's our Spanish blood – we tan easy. She is dark like me with the same black hair, except mine is long, hers is short.

The problem with staying onboard is that Mom says she doesn't like to see "idle hands". There is always a list of chores that she is keen to dish out to me.

"I'm going ashore," I said.

"Have you done your school work?" She didn't look up at me.

"Yes." I lied. I had a Spanish vocab test on Friday and I hadn't studied for it, but I could do that later. Being home-schooled, you can kind of keep your own timetable.

I stood on the deck of The *Phaedra* and looked at the island. I didn't need to take the Zodiac. It was only forty metres to shore and I could swim that far easy.

Mom wasn't totally joking when she said about me making the swim team. If I trained I could probably go to the Olympics. I can swim like a fish. Maybe better than some fishes. So Mom never worries about me.

I stepped out of my shorts and pulled off my T-shirt and stood on the edge of the boat in my bikini, staring down at the deep blue water. Then I raised my hands above my head and I dived.

The water was cooler than I expected. It shocked me and left me gasping a little as I broke the surface and began to swim for shore. Every ten or so strokes I raised my head right up to see how much further I had to swim. As I got nearer to the island, the jungle loomed dark and silent on the horizon. I was in mid-stroke when there was a violent eruption from the treetops. A flock of scarlet parrots suddenly took flight, flapping their lime-green wings, cawing and complaining loudly.

I stopped and trod water, listening to their cries echo through the bay. I couldn't see what had spooked them. I shielded my eyes with my hand against the glare of the sun on the water and peered out into the jungle. There! A shadow flickering through the trees. I felt a shiver down the back of my neck. I hesitated, and then put my head down and started swimming again.

Shipwreck Bay was shaped like a horseshoe and I swam my way right into the middle of the curve. In both directions white sand stretched on for about a hundred metres or so. My plan was to walk along the beach to the next bay and then all the way to the headland, which I figured would take about two hours – I would be back in time for dinner.

I set off, enjoying how my reef boots made alien footprints in the sand – with circles like octopus suckers on the soles and no toes. The parrots had gone silent, but I kept an eye on the trees all the same.

As I rounded the rocks to the next bay, I could see that my plan of walking to the headland wasn't going to work out. The bay ahead was sandy, the same as the one where we'd moored the *Phaedra*, but at the southern end there was a cliff-face that jutted all the way into the sea, too sheer to climb. If I wanted to keep going then I needed to turn inland.

As I pushed my way through black mangroves and waist-high marsh grass, the ground became squelchy underfoot. I hadn't gone far when I noticed an itching on my ankle and I looked down and saw this big, black leech stuck to my leg just above the rim of my reef boot.

If you ever need to pull a leech off, the thing you mustn't do is panic. If you rip them off, they will vomit into the wound and cause an infection. You need to use your fingernail to detach the sucker and ease the leech off.

I tried to use my fingernails, but I kept getting grossed out and pulling my hand away. I had finally got up the nerve to do it when the leech got so full and plump that it just plopped off of its own accord. I stomped down on it and felt sick as I watched my own blood oozing back out.

After that, every blade of grass against my shin made me jump. I kept imagining shiny black leeches attaching themselves to my flesh, looking for a warm pulse to plunge their teeth into.

As I got closer to the jungle the parrots started up again. They were shrieking from the tops of the Caribbean pines. *Look out!* their cries seemed to say. *Dangerous, dangerous!*

And then, another sound. Louder than the cries of the parrots. A crashing and crunching, the sound of something moving through the scrubby undergrowth beneath the pines.

I stood very still and listened hard. Whatever was in there, it was big and it was coming my way, moving fast.

From the sounds it made as it thundered towards

me, I figured it had to be a wild boar! They live in the jungles on most islands in the Bahamas and the islanders hunt them for meat. If you're hunting them, you have to make sure your aim is good because you don't want to wound them and make them angry. Boars can attack. They've got these long tusks that can kill you on the spot.

I looked around me for a tree to shimmy up, but it was all snakewood and pigeon berry, too spindly to take my weight. My heart was hammering at my chest. The boar must be close now, but there was nowhere to run. I scrambled around, trying to find a stick, something big and solid. The crashing was deafening, so near...

And then she appeared in the clearing in front of me.

It hurt me afterwards to think that the first time I ever saw her my reaction was to shrink back in fear. But like I said, I thought she was a boar. The last thing you ever expect to see in the jungle is a horse.

She had this stark white face, pale as bone, with these blue eyes staring out like sapphires set into china. Above her wild blue eyes her forelock was tangled with burrs and bits of twig so that it resembled those religious paintings of Jesus with a crown of thorns, and along her neck the mane had become so matted and tangled it had turned into dreadlocks.

Strange brown markings covered her ears, as if she was wearing a hat, and there were more brown splotches over her withers, chest and rump. The effect was like camouflage so that she blended into the trees and this made her white face appear even more ghoulish, as if it just floated there all on its own with those weird blue eyes. She was like some voodoo queen who had taken on animal form.

She didn't turn and run at the sight of me. It was as if she expected to find me there in the middle of the jungle.

She stood there for a minute, her nostrils flared, taking in my scent on the air. And then she took a step forward, moving towards me. I stepped backwards. I mean, I wasn't scared. It was just that she was nothing like those horses down the road back home in Florida. I had never seen a horse like this before. The way she held her head up high, imperious and proud, as if she owned the jungle.

The horse stretched out her neck, lowering her

white face towards me and I held my ground. I could feel her warm, misty breath on my skin. She was no ghost. She was flesh and blood like me. Slowly, I raised my hand so that the tips of my fingers brushed against the velvet of her muzzle and that was when I felt it. I know it made no sense but right there and then I knew that it was real and powerful and true. That this bold, beautiful arrogant creature was somehow *mine*.

And then the stupid parrots ruined everything. I don't know what startled them but suddenly the trees around us shook as they took flight, screeching.

I put out a hand to grasp her mane but it was too late. She surged forward, cutting so close to me that I could have almost flung my arms around her as she swept by, taking the path back the way I had just come through the mangroves.

Her legs were invisible beneath the thick waves of marsh grass, so that as she cantered away from me with her tail sweeping in her wake she looked like a ship ploughing through rough ocean, rising and cresting with each canter stride. And then she was free of the grass and galloping along the beach. I could see her pale limbs gathering up beneath her and plunging deep down into the sand. She held her head high as she ran and didn't look back. Her hoofbeats pounded out a rhythm as she rounded the curve at the other end of the cove. And then she was gone.

# Voodoo Queen

There was no way. I could catch her, but I ran after her all the same. I slogged through the mangroves and then back on to the beach.

By the time I reached our bay where the *Phaedra* was anchored she had disappeared. No hoofprints and no sign of her anywhere. The birds, who had been so full of noise, had gone eerily quiet.

I crouched with my hands on my knees to get my breath back, then I stood up and scanned the sand dunes for my horse. When I couldn't see her, I waded straight out into the sea. My strokes cut the water fast and clean all the way back to the *Phaedra*.

"Mom?"

She wasn't on deck.

"Mom!"

Mom ran up from below deck. "What's wrong? What is it?"

"I saw a horse."

The look of concern turned to annoyance. "Beatriz, this isn't funny. I am working."

"I'm not trying to be funny!" My chest was still heaving from the effort of my run and swim. I was having trouble getting the words out. "I saw a horse... just now."

"Being ridden on the beach?"

"No." I was still trying to breathe. "It was alone in the jungle and it was wild, but I patted it and then the birds scared it away."

Mom frowned. "You met a wild horse in the jungle that let you get close enough to pat it."

"Yes, well, almost."

"And what did this horse look like?"

"It had blue eyes and a white face and dreadlocks and this marking on its head like a hat..."

Mom looked hard at me.

"Mom, I'm not making it up... I can show you."

"The horse?"

"No," I shook my head. "She ran away but I can

show you the hoofprints. Not here. They washed away. But in the next bay there will be some."

"I really don't have time for this."

"It won't take long," I pleaded. "Come and see!"

"Beatriz," Mom's voice was firm, "I don't know where you think you are going with this horse business, but if this is part of your campaign to convince me to go back to Florida, I can tell you now that interrupting my work is going the wrong way about it."

"I'm not lying!"

"I never said you were lying, Beatriz…"

"Yes, you did!" I was furious now. Mom is always saying I have an overactive imagination – which is true, but that is totally different from telling lies. Also, people are always telling you to have big dreams – like going to the Olympics – and then they tell you off for being a dreamer. So which one is it?

"I tell you what," Mom said, "how about if I come and look for the hoofprints later, OK? We can go before dinner and have a walk on the beach and you can show me then."

"It'll be too late by dinner," I insisted. "The waves will have washed them away."

"Just give me an hour then," Mom said. "Once

I've done this migration chart we can go, OK? We'll take the Zodiac to the next bay and you can show me."

"OK…" I gave in. "One hour."

I stayed on deck staring out at the island while Mom worked downstairs, watching in case the horse reappeared.

*She was real*, I whispered, trying to convince myself. But she hadn't seemed real at first, had she? Did I actually touch her? My horse was like a ghost, a voodoo queen, and now she was disappearing, fading like a vapour as I waited for Mom and the next sixty minutes to tick past. And then another sixty. She was still working.

"I have about another half an hour to go," she insisted when I went downstairs.

And another half an hour after that.

"We'll go in the morning, OK?" Mom said as she served up dinner. She had made curried fish with coconut cream and rice – which is usually my favourite, but I wasn't eating, just poking it around the plate.

"Sure," I said in a flat voice. "Great, Mom."

I lay in bed that night and looked up at the horse posters on my wall. I guess it is true that I have a vivid imagination. When I lived in Florida I had lots of imaginary horses. I made them all bridles out of rope with their names on bits of cardboard and I hung them up in the garden shed and pretended that was my tack room.

This was back when I was friends with Kristen. She was a horsey girl too. She would come over after school and we would showjump. We'd leap over fences made out of broomsticks and paint cans in the backyard. We didn't always go clear – sometimes our horses would refuse, or knock a rail down and get faults. But I knew all the time that those horses weren't real. And I could never have made up a horse like the one that I had seen in the jungle. I had never seen a horse like that in my life.

Well, if Mom wanted proof then she would get it.

Looking back, I guess I should have left a note. At the time I thought it would only make Mom angry if I told her what I was doing. I would have acted differently if I had only known what lay ahead.

# The Mudpit

I'd got my clothes ready before I went to bed so that I could sneak out of the bunk room early the next morning and get dressed on deck without waking Mom. I'd already loaded my supplies – a bottle of water, a knife, some rope, a cheese sandwich (for me) and an apple (for the horse) – into my backpack and I threw the pack in first then climbed down the ladder and into the Zodiac.

I didn't want to make a noise with the outboard motor so I rowed the Zodiac to shore. I'm OK at rowing, but I do end up going in circles sometimes. Luckily it was an incoming tide so that made it easier. When I reached the beach, I had to drag the inflatable all the way above the high tidemark so that the waves couldn't pick it up and wash it away. I made sure Mom could see it from the *Phaedra* – I figured she could always swim over if she needed it while I was gone. Then I strapped on my backpack and headed inland, walking in the direction that the horse had gone, tracing her path from yesterday, following her into the jungle.

Beneath the dark canopy of the trees, the jungle floor was a tangle of snakewood and sea grape. I was looking for signs that the horse had been this way. You know, like they always do in movies, where they find a broken branch and then they know that the fugitive they are tracking has been there? Only I couldn't see any broken branches, so I just kept walking.

As I pushed my way through the undergrowth, I thought about the horse, the way her mane had been tangled with burrs. If she really belonged to someone then you'd think they would have brushed her. The way I figured it, she must have been roaming loose for a long time. Maybe she didn't even have an owner at all. I remembered that feeling I had when our eyes met, like we were bonded together somehow. *My horse.*

"You have an overactive imagination, Beatriz," I muttered.

What I didn't have was much sense of direction. As I walked deeper into the jungle I was beginning to wonder if I would be able to find my way back to the *Phaedra* again. When I had looked on the map, the island hadn't seemed that big. I thought it would have taken me maybe half an hour to walk all the way across. But I had been walking that long already and I was still in dense jungle.

All the time as I walked, I had been listening to the birdsong, but now I heard another noise. In the trees to the left of me – the sound of branches snapping and crackling underfoot. I couldn't see anything, but I had this feeling – like I was being stalked. Something or someone was in the trees with me, watching me, keeping their movements in step with my own. If I stopped walking, then it was quiet, but then when I set off again, I could have sworn I heard something.

"Who's there?"

There was no reply.

I changed direction, heading away from the noises, walking faster, pushing my way through the trees.

I fought my way through the snakewood and pigeon berry and suddenly found myself in this vast clearing. I felt like I'd stumbled into a magical realm.

The undergrowth disappeared completely, and there was a perfect circle of bare earth. At the centre of the circle was a massive tree. Its branches spread out in all directions, with sturdy limbs that were the perfect cradle for a secret tree house. The trunk was broad, with deep crevices, like folds in a curtain that you could have hidden yourself inside, and the roots stretched out like gnarled hands clawing into the earth.

I sat down on one of those roots, leant against the trunk and opened my backpack. I took out the sandwich and ate that and drank about half of the water in my bottle. Then I pulled out the rope and made a horse's halter. I hadn't ever used a real halter so I just fashioned it like the ones for my imaginary horses back in Florida, with a piece to go over the nose and another piece behind the ears – but big enough for a real horse obviously. I am good at sailor's knots from being on the *Phaedra* so it looked quite sturdy once I was done.

I slung the halter over my shoulder and then I closed my eyes and I listened. I could hear the birdcalls, I could hear the leaves rustling above me, but there was also another sound – gentle, persistent, pounding in my head.

*I could hear the sea.*

I knew where to go now. The jungle began to thin out as the sea sound grew closer. On the other side of the island, the beach was quite different from Shipwreck Bay. The coast was one vast expanse of mudflats. Forests of mangroves sprouted up out of murky, shallow seawater pools, the remnants of the last tide that had been trapped and left behind.

I pushed my way through the tangles of mangroves and then stopped dead. Right in front of me in the middle of the mudflats, grazing on the marsh grass, was my horse.

*She was real.* And she was just as strange-looking as I'd remembered. With her crazy dreadlocked mane and her weird markings – the white face with the brown sunhat over her ears. But she was beautiful too. She had a pretty dish to her nose and a crest to her neck that made her look refined and elegant despite her bedraggled state. I thought about the way she had looked at me, when she first saw me in the forest, like she was queen of the island. There was that same nobility about her, even now as she stood fetlock-deep in the muddy waters, ripping up mouthfuls of the unappetising marsh tussock.

All the time I was walking, I had been planning

what I'd do when I found her. My idea was to use the apple in my backpack to tempt her and then I would put the halter on. No, I am not joking – that was my plan. I can see how mad it was now, but the first time I met her, I had been so near, I figured I could easily get that close again and then the apple would do all the work.

Some plan. At the sound of me splashing and stumbling my way towards her through the mud she startled like a gazelle.

"No – don't go!"

I wrestled frantically with my backpack, yanking it open to pull out the apple, but it was useless. She was gone already – galloping off across the mudflats, her tail held up high like a banner behind her, great splashes of seawater flinging up beneath her belly as she thundered across the mud.

I didn't even try to run after her this time. She was way ahead of me, and she was so fast! I watched her, marvelling at her beauty, the way her legs gathered up and then drove back to earth again all at once, working like pistons powering her on.

And then, halfway across the mudflats, for some reason her strides slowed. She began to lumber along, her legs moving in an ungainly way, and then suddenly, out of nowhere, she fell. She went down hard and the way she lurched so violently reminded me of a zebra being taken down by a lion in a nature documentary.

As she struggled to right herself and get back up on her feet, I noticed that her hindquarters had almost completely disappeared into the mud. And that was when I realised. She hadn't been taken down. The ground beneath had given way.

I thought she would fight her way free and get back to her feet. But she couldn't seem to get out of the mud. She was flailing about, thrashing with her front legs. She got herself right up on her haunches, rearing up out of the sand, but then plunged back down again, rolling and twisting to one side as she fell.

I ran out on to the mudflats, dropping my backpack halfway across. It was like those dreams you have where your legs are stuck in glue and you can't lift them and everything goes into slow motion. The mud suctioned at my feet, dragging at my legs. I was fighting for every stride. My breath came in panicked, desperate gasps.

My poor horse was going totally crazy. She lurched and faltered so that her neck swung like a pendulum, her head smacking down hard into the mud with a sickening thud. She was trapped, and struggling was only making it worse.

I kept running to her until I felt the ground beneath my feet go really soft. From here on in I had to test the ground with each step. I circled right round the horse, padding as I stepped, trying to find the best spot to approach from, where the ground was more solid.

My horse was foaming with sweat and shaking all over. She didn't seem scared of me though; she was too focused on fighting her way out of the mud. I could see the whites of her eyes showing at the edges, making her blue eyes look even wilder. I could feel my heart hammering, but I had to get closer if I was going to help her, so I kept edging forward. I'd only taken a couple of steps when I felt the mud beneath me give way. I let out a squeal and the horse stopped thrashing and looked at me. *Stay calm*, I told myself, *you can do this*. I was almost close enough to reach her.

I ploughed on and felt the ground devouring me with each step. Then my foot got stuck and I collapsed hard against her.

The horse swung her neck as I fell, trying to move

away from me, but she had nowhere to go. I grasped her soaking wet mane and clung on to it.

"I'm sorry," I said. I tried to push myself back off her but I was stuck. Her shoulder was pressed up hard against my thigh and I sank further into the mud.

"Easy, girl. Stay calm. I'm going to get you out."

I still had the rope halter slung over my shoulder. With fumbling hands I tried to slip the loop over her nose and then I lifted the earpiece over her head. She didn't flinch from my touch. It was like she knew I was trying to help her.

Once I got the halter on, the hard work really began. It took me ages to pull myself back out of the mud. I would work one leg free only to have it suctioned back down as I fought to loosen the other limb. In the end I managed to crawl free by clawing my way out with my hands, using my fingers like grappling hooks to pull myself out. At least I knew that I could get free again if I needed to. But while I was light enough to get out of the mud hole, my horse wasn't. And the more she struggled, the deeper she sank.

I moved round so that I was facing her, and then, grasping on with one hand each side of the rope halter, I leant back with all my weight, dug in my heels and I pulled. I pulled with all my strength, as hard as I could.

And… Nothing. The only thing that happened was I began sinking faster than before back into the mud.

I tried again, really yanking at the halter so that the ropes dug into the horse's face. But even as I tried again I knew it wasn't going to work. The horse must have weighed at least ten times as much as me and she was stuck deep.

I looked around me for something I could use – a stick or a branch. But there was nothing except marsh grass and tidal pools. And the sea. The sea, which, as I now noticed, was getting closer. *The tide was coming in.*

This whole mudflat must end up underwater when the tide was high. *My horse would end up underwater.* I searched more desperately for something to pull her out with. And then, when I couldn't find anything, I began to dig. Maybe I could make a channel through the mud so that she could fight her way back to the surface again.

I used both hands, scooping up the sand through my legs like a dog. There was a frenzy to my digging as I shovelled the mud up and threw it aside, and

I flung myself into the task, digging the channel as fast as I could. With every handful of mud that I dug up, more mud oozed in to take its place. All I was doing was making the hole more and more squishy and unstable.

I tried to dig closer to the horse, and felt the mud cave away completely so that I was up to my thighs once more.

It was futile to try and get her out. So instead, I made up my mind that I would stay with her for as long as possible. She struggled less if I stayed close and stroked her, spoke soothing words to her. I could drag myself out when the time came, but until that moment I would not abandon her.

"It's OK." I cradled her head. "It's going to be OK." But I believed this less and less. She was exhausted and so was I. The sun was right overhead and it was hot, really hot. My head was throbbing, and I felt prickly all over, like my skin had hot needles pressing into it.

I became mesmerised by the lapping of the sea, the way it kept creeping forward, slowly but surely. We had another hour left at most before it reached us.

"I'm sorry," I kept saying to my horse. Because I

knew now that I couldn't save her. But I couldn't leave her. Not yet.

Maybe it was the sun that made me dizzy, I don't know, but at some point I must have begun slipping in and out of consciousness. I would wake up with a jolt and then sink back into a dream.

*Get up*, I told myself. *Things have gone too far now.* It was time to get myself out of the mud. It probably sounds weird to say I was freezing, because the sun was right up overhead, but suddenly I felt chilled to the bone.

It was when I realised that I couldn't move my legs that I truly began to panic. They'd gone completely numb under the mud. I tried to kick and felt myself sink deeper.

I clawed at the mud, driven on by raw adrenaline, but even the fear wasn't enough to bring the strength back to my exhausted arms. My muscles were jelly.

"Help me!" The words came out weak and strangled. My throat was thick and dry, my tongue swollen. "Help me!"

I swear the parrots laughed at me. I heard them *caw-caw*. Why were they so horrible?

"Help me…" My words were choked with tears. I was so stupid. *I should have left Mom a note.* What if she never ever found me? I didn't want to die out here in the middle of nowhere. I didn't want to die.

My head was all woozy. I shut my eyes to block out the glare and my world became darkness and sounds. There was the constant lap and swell of the sea as it crept up on me, and the birds calling in the sky above us, the rattle of the horse's breath and the mud gurgling beneath me. And then, cutting through all of these, I heard a shrill whine, like a mosquito at first, then growing closer and louder until it filled my ears. I opened my eyes and squinted into the sun.

It was a motorbike.

# A Shadow on the Sun

The horse had lost all her fight. She lay submerged in the mud beside me, each rattling, heaving gasp she took seeming like it might be her last. Then the motorbike roared into the silence and brought her violently back to her senses.

She began to thrash about, legs flailing in the mud alongside me. I felt one of her front hooves accidentally glance against the hard bone of my ankle and I swallowed the pain in a wrenching gasp of agony. Trying to get away from her, I uselessly clawed at the mud again. But I had no strength left.

I tried to cry out again, to say, "I'm here!" but my tongue had turned to rubber. The motorbike noise filled my head, piercing my brain.

And then it stopped.

I could see a figure walking towards me. I screwed my face up against the blinding glare. My eyes hurt so much I had to shut them tight. When I opened them there was a shadow looming above me, blocking out the sun.

"My goodness, child! How long is you been like dis?"

I squinted up at the silhouette.

"I don't know," I replied. "Hours, I guess." I could barely get the words out of my dry mouth. I was still sun-blind but when the figure bent down really low, putting her face near mine, I could see that it was a woman. She had dark coffee-coloured skin and her hair was matted in dreadlocks, tangled with grey. She had a thick, broad nose, and swollen lips. Her eyes stared into mine with a keen brightness.

"Here." She held my head by the chin and pushed a water bottle to my lips. "Drink it."

I took five or six deep gulps. I had to fight with my own tongue to get the water down. It felt amazing.

I drank again and the woman grunted her approval, then put the empty bottle back in the bag she'd slung over her shoulder. She stood up and her

53

shadow, which had mercifully blocked out the sun, was gone. I shut my eyes against the sun's glare and when I opened them again I could see her walking away.

"No! Don't leave! No!"

The motorbike engine cranked back to life. She was driving away!

I shouted until my throat was raw. But she didn't come back. Soon, I couldn't even hear the bike any more.

I willed the old woman to return. But there was no sound except the lapping of the waves growing nearer and the cries of the seabirds spiralling in the sky. In my mind the birds became vultures, circling above, waiting for the life to ebb out of us. When a gull landed right in front of me I screamed and reeled back in fright.

"Go away!" I shouted, grabbing a handful of mud and throwing it as hard as I could. "Leave us alone!"

That was when I broke down and cried. My breath came in horrible hiccups, as I choked on my sobs.

I washed in and out of consciousness and when I was awake it all felt like a dream. I honestly don't know how long it was before I heard the sound of an engine again. Not a whine this time, but a full-bodied roar. In the distance something big was rumbling across the mudflats. I shielded my eyes with my hands. It was an old farm tractor, ancient rusty red, but the old woman drove it like it was a racing car, speeding across the mudflats, flinging a sheet of water up in her wake.

When she reached us she swung round wide so she wouldn't disturb the mud hole. Then the tractor engine went dead and the next thing I knew she was standing right there next to me.

"You got a name, child?"

"Beatriz." I managed to get the word out through my swollen, sunburnt lips. "My name is Beatriz Ortega."

"Well, Bee-a-trizz child, I be Annie." She thrust a ragged bit of frayed rope at me. "Take it!" she insisted. "You needs to get your hand under de horse's belly. You'll have to dig de mud, Bee-a-trizz, dig hard."

"I can't do it!" I was weeping as I said it. My fingernails were already raw from trying to dig the horse out and my arms were too weak.

"Yes, you can, child," Annie said firmly. "Come on now!"

Annie went back to the tractor and grabbed a shovel and then she came and began to dig on the other side of the horse. She was making a hole for me to poke the rope through. "Come on, Bee-a-trizz. Not much more... keep goin'."

I dug until my fingers bled, tears running down my cheeks.

"Dat's de way!" Annie encouraged me. "You is doin' it, Bee-a-trizz child! We almost dere..."

And then I felt her fingers clasp my own and she had the rope in her hands. She pulled it beneath the horse's belly and then knotted it across the horse's back, taking another length, which she crossed through and ran round the horse's hindquarters. I lay my face down on the mud, utterly exhausted.

"You got to do another tink for me, Bee-a-trizz."

Annie passed the rope to me again. "Tie it off by her belly and we is done. Tie a strong knot, make it tight."

I plunged my hands back into the mud once more. I did the knot by feel, tying it blind beneath the mud. My hands were so weak and numb it took forever, but I managed it. The rope now ran right the way round the horse's belly, closing the circuit and creating a harness.

Annie checked the knots and grunted with satisfaction. Then she came over and bent down on all fours and clasped me under the armpits.

"Hang on to me, child!" she commanded. I was shaking so badly I could hardly grip. "Get a good strong hold!" Annie snapped at me. "You gots to be ready when I pull. You cling to me, child, and you stay dead still. Ain't gonna do no good if you kick about."

With her arms wrapped round me, Annie crouched low and then she took a deep breath and strained. With a firm, sudden yank she heaved me out and dragged me clear of the mud hole. For an old woman she was plenty strong! I lay on the sand, gasping like a fish that had just been landed on a dock.

She dragged me up the beach a little way and then gave me another bottle of water to drink and went back to her tractor. Humming to herself, she got behind the wheel and revved the engine. The tractor lurched forward and the ropes went taut. Then suddenly the tractor tyres began to spin, straining against the weight. The tractor was going backwards, being dragged into the hole, falling in on top of the horse!

Annie didn't seem concerned. Still humming, she

cranked up the gears and put her foot down. The engine revved and, in fits and starts, the tractor edged forward. As it did so, my horse seemed to stir back to life. Reawakened, she began flailing with her forelegs.

The tractor had loosened the mud's grip and with a dramatic scramble of limbs, the horse lurched forward. She came halfway out so that her front legs were visible above the mud. She only needed to get her haunches out and she would be free. But her legs didn't seem able to move any further. They had gone weak and numb from their hours thrashing beneath the mud. When Annie finally dragged her up so that she was almost standing, the horse wobbled as her hind legs collapsed. She was going to fall back into the hole!

Annie was ready for her. She let the horse find her feet, ignoring the seawater that had begun to fill the hole and the tractor tyres rapidly sinking down into the mud.

Then the tractor gave a loud growl as Annie suddenly gunned it forward and the horse was catapulted clear out of the mud hole.

I watched in horror as my horse stumbled and fell to its knees. For a sickening moment I thought she might break a leg, but Annie kept the ropes taut so that the horse managed to go forward in a series of awkward stumbles until it stood at last on firm ground.

Annie dug a handkerchief out of the sleeve of her dirty floral dress and used it to mop the sweat off her brow. Now that the horse was out, she had a look of utter relief on her face as she jumped down off the tractor.

The horse didn't flinch at Annie's touch. She stood weak as a kitten while Annie ran her hands over her and then untied the ropes and refastened them to the halter and hitched the horse to the back of the tractor.

"She be OK," she said, nodding sagely. "Notink broken. Just some scratches is all." Then she looked me over. "Bee-a-trizz," she said, "look at you shakin'! You gonna catch youself ammonia from bein' in dat hole. You be comin' home wit' me."

Annie helped me up on to the tractor so that I was sitting on the wheel arch of one of the massive tyres.

"I want to go home," I said. My voice sounded weird to me – so small, so pitiful. Annie didn't even seem to hear me – or at least she didn't say anything.

She clambered up to take her place at the steering wheel in front of me and put the tractor into gear.

And so, with the horse following behind the tractor, and me perched up there on the wheel arch, Annie chugged slowly back across the mudflats. Not towards home, but in the opposite direction, away from Mom and the *Phaedra*, towards the dark jungle hills of Great Abaco.

# Annie's Crib

"**M**y boat is in the other direction... please..."
It was useless. Annie didn't even acknowledge my words. She just kept driving, humming away to herself.

The ride got even bumpier when we left the mudflats and took the wide dirt track that cut up through the jungle hills. The horse stumbled on behind the tractor on wobbly legs, doing her best to keep up and I clung on, flung about with every pothole and rut we struck.

I was still feeling really woozy and I was about to beg Annie to stop when she cut the engine and said, "We is here."

'Here' was a bright yellow and turquoise beach

cottage, a tiny hideaway with its front porch poking out from beneath the trees. To the side of the cottage there was a rusted-out old car wreck, and beside it some makeshift wooden pens that looked like they were used to house animals, although they were empty at the moment. The only living creatures were three scrawny brown chickens roaming free and a painfully thin white cat who ran at the sight of us. A tinkling like wind chimes came from a tree in the middle of the front yard, its branches strung with beer bottles. Annie caught me staring at the bottle tree and gave a cackle.

"Dey for keepin' away de evil."

Annie jumped off the tractor and helped me down from the wheel rim.

"I want to go home," I mumbled weakly as she lifted me to the ground. I felt like a four-year-old begging for Mommy. Annie paid me no attention. She just walked up to the front porch and I had no choice but to follow her.

The porch floorboards were so old they bent dangerously beneath my feet. Tangles of chicken bones and purple herbs were bound in knotted red twine and strung from the eaves, and I had to duck underneath to get inside.

Most places look huge to me after living on the *Phaedra*, but not Annie's house. The whole place was just three tiny rooms. The living room was so cramped there was barely space for Annie, me and the sofa to all be there at once. Through an open doorway was the kitchen. It was no more than a campfire stove, a sink and a wooden table and chairs. The bedroom was even smaller, with a single bed that seemed to touch all four walls at once.

The smallness felt more extreme because it was like Annie had taken knick-knacks from a house three times the size and crammed them all in. There were more bundles of purple herbs hanging from hooks, and shelves stacked with animal skeletons, conch shells and ebony figurines. A wooden carving of grimacing faces took pride of place on the wall above the kitchen table. The lightshades looked like they were made from animal skins, and crazy hand-painted beaded curtains were strung across the bedroom doorway.

I stood in the living room, soaked to the skin, dripping mud on to Annie's rag-cloth rug and shaking so badly I could barely control my limbs.

"Take your clothes off," Annie instructed. I began to slowly peel off my wet things while Annie swished through the beaded curtain and dug around in a chest of drawers. She returned with a faded old yellow T-shirt that said, "Smile – You're in the Bahamas!" in bright green letters and a pair of shorts with palm trees on them.

Annie handed me the clothes. "Dey ain't best-best. Yard clothes is all I got."

While I got dressed, Annie rinsed my things in the kitchen sink. Then she threw my clothes in a plastic basin and headed back out of the front door. "You stay here," she instructed.

I watched out of the window as Annie pegged my things on the washing line. Then she went back to the tractor and untied my horse and led her round the side of the house to the animal pens. The horse seemed to follow her quietly and obediently, so maybe she wasn't so wild after all. Or maybe, like me, she was just too tired to put up a fight. I guess I could have tried to run away right then while Annie was outside, but I didn't think I could find my way back to the *Phaedra* from here on my own, and it was getting dark.

I flopped down on Annie's threadbare old sofa. The whole room smelt of those weird purple herbs. My head was still swimming and I was freezing cold despite the dry clothes. I lay down and shut my eyes. I felt like I was going to throw up.

64

"You al' right?" Annie was standing over me.

"Yeah," I managed weakly.

"You tirsty?" she asked. I nodded.

It only took three steps for Annie to reach the kitchen.

She poured a glass of something from the plastic pitcher in the fridge and handed it to me.

I gave it a suspicious sniff.

"Switcher," she said. "You drink. It be good for you."

I took a nervous sip and then gave in to my desperate thirst and gulped it down greedily. The tang of lime juice and sugar-cane sweetness stung my parched throat. Annie took the empty glass back. "You want more?"

"Yes... please."

She refilled the glass then went back to the fridge. The room was spinning worse than ever but I took a deep breath and then I swung my legs round and planted my feet on the floor.

"I really need to go home," I said weakly. "Please can you take me home?"

Annie looked at me; her face was stony. "State of you? You ain't goin' nowhere."

"My mom... she'll be worried..." As I said this,

I tried to stand up and keeled over, my legs collapsing clean away beneath me.

"Lord above, child!" Annie exclaimed as she helped me up again on to the sofa. She felt my forehead with the back of her hand. "No wonder you all fainty! You is burnin' hot! You done got heatstroke!"

She swept through the bead curtains and grabbed the blankets off her bed and threw them over me. They did nothing to warm me. I was chilled to the bone and shaking uncontrollably. Annie tucked me in and propped another pillow under my head, then sat down on the sofa beside me. My head throbbed and everything was woozy. I felt a hand stroke my brow.

"Mom?" I murmured. "Mommy?"

My head was swimming; I couldn't think straight. The light in the room suddenly seemed unbearable, far too bright. I closed my eyes and let the darkness soothe me...

*Then I opened them again and the brightness was gone. Not just the brightness. Everything. I took a deep breath and found myself gasping for air.*

Breathe! *I told myself.* Just little breaths – in and out. Stay calm and breathe.

*My hands went to touch my waist and I almost lost my breath with shock as I felt a gap where my waist should be. There was something crushing my stomach, holding me so tight that it was choking my ribcage. I looked down and saw that it was a corset made from sapphire-blue velvet, stitched and boned with silk ribbons.*

*I smoothed the velvet down with my hands and as I did so I caught a glimpse of my toes poking out below the hem of my gown.*

*My feet were bare and I could feel the chill of cobblestones beneath them.*

*I raised my head, my eyes adjusted now to the gloom. Ahead of me in the half-light I could make out arched porticos and the high vaulted ceiling above, and a long corridor stretching out ahead of me with wooden doors on each side. I could smell the sweet, fetid aroma of manure and hear the stamp and whicker of the horses all around me.*

*And at that moment I was certain of one thing.*

*I wasn't in Annie's front room any more.*

# If They Catch You . . .

It must have been a dream. But even now that I am back onboard the *Phaedra*, I swear that it was not. If it was a dream then why can I remember every sensation, every smell and sound as if I were really there?

*I could feel the hard, cold cobbles beneath my feet, my skirts swishing at my ankles as I hurried along the corridor. I felt my heart pounding and my lungs breathless — due in part to the crushing tightness of the corset, but also to my overwhelming fear. I was afraid because I knew they were coming for me.*

If they catch you, they will kill you.

*These words had been spoken to me once as a warning and I knew them to be true.*

I began to run, the bag slung across my back bouncing hard against my spine with every stride.

In these grand stables there were over fifty stalls and the one that I sought was right at the very end. When I reached it at last I fell upon the door, working the bolt with shaking hands, sliding it open and stepping inside.

"Cara!" I hissed her name in the gloom. There was a dark shadow in the corner of the loose box and when I spoke it moved towards me.

"Cara?"

The black silhouette stepped out from the shadows and at last I saw her face, so haughty and regal, and those blue eyes, as clear as the sky.

"My Cara Blanca!" I threw my arms round her and hugged her as hard as I could. She nickered and shook her mane as I held her. She too was overjoyed by our reunion. But our hugs were brief and then I threw the bag on to the straw floor.

"Cara, they are right behind me. We do not have much time!"

With my horse standing beside me I began to undress, pulling at the bindings of my costume, my fingers tearing at the silk ribbon that held the brutal corset so tightly against my chest. My velvet dress fell to the floor. My old 'self' to be abandoned from this moment on.

*I dropped to my knees in the darkness and began my transformation.*

*From the tangle of garments in my bag I pulled out the roll of mutton cloth that I had stolen from the royal kitchen. It was gauzy and as stretchy as a bandage and it did the trick perfectly as I bound it round my chest, like a mummy being wrapped for the tomb.*

*With each bind of the cloth, I became as hard and flat-chested as a boy.*

*Over this I pulled on a shirt made of rough cotton and a coarse woollen waistcoat in drab grey. I pulled on my father's trousers — they were too large for me, but I cinched them in with a belt and tucked them into his riding boots. Then I shoved my gown and my velvet headpiece strung with pearls into the bag and moved over to the window.*

*Through the iron bars I looked out at the orange trees, heavy with brilliant fruit, the porticos draped with bougainvillea flowers, and my heart broke. This would be the last time I would watch the sun rise on the beauty of the Alhambra. This was over for me. Never again would I see Spain.*

*"There is nothing here for me now," I murmured to my horse. "All I have in the world is you and they will not take you from me. I will do whatever I must for us to be together. If I cannot change the mind of the Queen then I must change my own fate instead..."*

*Right at the bottom of the bag there was a leather-bound book, stamped in gold with my initials. Tucked in beside this was what I was searching for — a pair of shears. I clasped the handle and withdrew them, holding them in the dawn light so that the sun glinted off the steel. I looked at Cara standing so trustingly before me. She didn't know that I was doing this for her, out of love. I ran my finger down the edge, testing the blade. So this was it then. Once I made the first cut there would be no turning back...*

*Footsteps!*

*They were coming. They were echoing down the corridor. I couldn't tell how many of them there were but more than three men, maybe four or five or more.*

*I raised the metal blade in my right hand. In just a few moments they would be upon me. Even if I wanted to change my mind it was too late...*

*Suddenly the door swung open and I was bathed in light, blinding overwhelming light, and then there was a voice and it was calling my name.*

*My* other *name.*

Bee-a-trizz, Bee-a-trizz...

# Medicine Hat

Annie pulled the curtains back and in an instant the world of those dark Spanish stables fell away. The light poured in, brightening the front room where I lay on Annie's sofa and I was myself once more. The same me that I had been before, curled beneath the blankets, my bedclothes damp with fever.

"Bee-a-trizz," Annie was saying. "Wake up, child! You been gone asleep forever. It be day-clean and the sun is up and I done made grits and you needs to eat."

I propped myself up and took the plate from Annie. My mind was spinning. Here I was, sitting on Annie's sofa with a plate of hot grits in my hands, so how could it be that a moment ago I had been in ancient Spain?

I was dazed and bewildered, but I was also starving. I ate a whole plateful of Annie's grits, and then another. I was too busy eating to say a word as I wolfed it down.

"Child, you must been dying fa' hungry," Annie shook her head in wonder as she dished up thirds.

This time though, she hesitated before she handed me the plate.

"How come you out alone on de mudflats?" Annie asked.

"I was following my horse," I said. "I found her yesterday in the jungle…"

"Ain't you who find de Medicine Hat," Annie shook her head. "Medicine Hat be lookin' for you."

"Medicine Hat?"

"Dat be what de horse is, child," Annie said. "A Medicine Hat. Dey call her dat on accounts of her markings – like a hat on her head. It make her special. A Medicine Hat be real good obeah. Good magic."

I chewed down another mouthful of grits. "So it's good luck getting stuck in a mud hole?"

Annie grunted. "You is alive, ain't you?"

73

She looked at me, her black eyes burning with intensity. "Everytink happen for a reason, child. You wait and see."

I put down the plate. I was beginning to feel sick again. "Can you take me back to my boat?" I asked. "My mom will be worried about me," I said. "She'll probably call the coastguard or something."

Annie smiled, as if she knew I was bluffing. Then she turned her back on me, and took my plate over to the kitchen sink. "You rest now, child. Den we see…"

I don't know if Annie put something weird in those grits but I was real sleepy after I ate. I must have dozed off for a little while, but I didn't dream this time and when I woke my own clothes were on the bed beside me. They'd been washed and dried out but they were all ripped and stained from my struggles in the mud hole.

I got dressed and went outside to find Annie. She was round the side of the cottage by the animal pens, using a plastic bottle to pour water into a washing machine tub that was serving as a water trough in the corner of the pen.

And there was my horse! She looked so much better than she had done when we arrived yesterday.

Her ears were pricked forward and her blue eyes were bright once more.

Annie had tied her off to the railing and now she began to smear her hind legs and rump with a tub of strange gooey greenish paste. It smelt disgusting.

"What's that stuff?" I frowned.

"White sage and banana leaf," Annie explained. "It heal de burns."

"Are you a vet?" I asked.

Annie laughed. "Mercy no, child! Ain't no vetery-nary been teaching me how to mix de potion!"

She continued to smear the paste over the raw marks on the horse's hindquarters where the ropes had cut her flesh. The mare flinched but she didn't kick out.

"De Duchess be al'right," Annie said, giving the mare a slappy pat on her rump.

"The Duchess?"

Annie looked at me as if I should have known already.

"Sure. Her name be de Duchess. Dis horse she be a very fancy lady."

Annie wiped off her hands on a rag. "In a day or two, maybe t'ree, de Duchess be ready to go back to de herd."

"So there are other horses on the island?" It hadn't occurred to me that my horse might have a family.

"Once, was a time when de herd was strong," Annie said. "Tirty-five horses or more. Den de hurricanes come and it bad-bad. De herd got small. Dere be maybe six or seven horse left..." Annie gestured with her lips. "This one, de Duchess, she be de only Medicine Hat. She be special above all de rest."

So Annie already knew this horse! It made sense, the way the mare let Annie handle her. Even so, I was crushed.

"Is she yours?" I tried to keep a bitter tone of disappointment out of my voice.

Annie shook her head. "De Duchess she is wild. Ain't nobody owns any horse here on Abaco."

I wasn't convinced. "She seems to know you."

Annie laughed. "Sure 'nuff she should know me!" she said. "I spend my whole life here lookin' out for dem horse. I feed dem, I try to keep dem safe. You not believe what dem Conchy Joes do to dem horse. Hunters dey shoot dem. Tourists come and chase 'em so dey can get close and take picture. Dem poor horse scared half to death. No wonder dem belly ain't got no foal..."

Annie let the sentence trail off and then as if a thought had just occurred to her, she squared up to me, her face so close to mine I could see the green flecks in her black eyes. "You have a dream last night, child?"

*How did she know?*

I stepped away from her.

"I want to go home," I stated again. "My mom will be worried about me."

Annie grunted. "Soon enough," she said. "Now you come back inside. Annie got sometink to show you."

I didn't want to go back in the cottage, but what choice did I have? Even if I had known how to get back to the *Phaedra* from here I wasn't strong enough to do it alone. I was still pretty woozy to tell the truth.

Inside, I watched as Annie scuttled over to the shelves where the skeleton bones and conch shells were arranged. There was a small stack of books there too and from this stack she withdrew a bundle of rags. Inside them was a thick book, bound in ancient brown leather. When she passed it to me, I saw the initials on the front, the letters *F* and *M* stamped in battered gold type, and felt a shock of recognition.

It was the same book that I had seen in my dream!

"Bee-a-trizz, can you divine it?" Annie asked. The way she said this, it made me figure that maybe she didn't know how to read. But then I opened the first page of the book and I realised what she meant.

"This book is written in Spanish."

Annie looked pleased, as if I had just confirmed something she already knew.

She pointed to the lettering on the opening page, which I held in my hands.

*El Diario de Felipa Molina*

Felipa Molina – *F* and *M*. My breath quickened and I felt for a moment as if I was once more bound in a corseted velvet gown, my feet padding through the cold stone cobbled corridors of the stables in ancient Spain.

"It's not a book exactly," I said. "It's a diary."

Annie grunted. "So, child? You can read?"

"Yes," I said. "Yes, I can…"

# The Diary of Felipa Molina

## 13th January, 1492

I write these words sitting in a cramped room above a highway inn on the outskirts of Cadiz. It is late at night and beneath my lodgings I can hear the men in the tavern carousing and carrying on like fools. I do not dare venture downstairs to ask the kitchen to make me something to eat – even though I am half starved.

I did not want to rest here, but I had no choice. Poor Cara was too exhausted to make the return journey to Granada.

Is it any wonder that my horse cannot go on? We rode like conquistadors today, galloping for almost five miles. At times, when the distance seemed too great and Cara was flagging, I would urge her on, whispering in her ear, "Cara

Blanca, show me your speed and prove to me your noble blood. Run as hard as you can, my beauty. For we have been entrusted with this mission by Queen Isabella and we shall not fail her."

In truth, though, it is not the Queen's idea that I am here. It is Princess Joanna – with her wicked sense of humour and her taste for trouble.

I was sitting at Joanna's side this morning when Christopher Columbus made his grand entrance to the royal court.

They say that Señor Columbus has the proud and noble profile of a falcon, but Joanna has other words for it.

"Here we go," Joanna whispered as she watched him stride past us towards the throne. "Old bird-nose is back!"

I had to bite my fist to stifle my laughter and Columbus shot me such a glare!

I had to lower my head so that I did not meet his eyes and could compose myself. It is not proper to laugh at a man while he meets with the Queen.

This was Columbus's second audience with Her Majesty. Once more he had come to ask for support for his plan to sail halfway across the world!

"It is a wonder my mother is willing to listen to him bore on again with his mad plans," Joanna muttered under her breath. "When I am queen you can be sure I will not bother to entertain such nonsense."

"Careful – you are not queen yet," I reminded her with a grin.

"No, but I am the Princess," Joanna shot back, "so best you hold your tongue!"

She smiled as she said this, but I detected a royal sting to her words.

Joanna is only fourteen years old, the same age as me, but already there is talk of her marriage. There are rumours that she is to become betrothed to Philip of Burgundy and Joanna is quite excited about this. Philip's nickname is 'Philip the Handsome'.

"Perhaps they are being sarcastic?" I teased her. "Perhaps Philip the Handsome has a hunchback and a nose like a turnip."

"No!" Joanna told me gaily. "I have seen a portrait and he is handsome indeed!"

Joanna is beautiful too. Like her mother Queen Isabella she has long dark blonde hair and blue eyes. I am the opposite of her – black hair and brown eyes – but inside our hearts we are like sisters. My mother, Teresa, was a companion to the Queen when she was a girl and now I serve the same role for Princess Joanna.

Lately, the Queen has insisted that Joanna must be present for all the goings-on in the royal court. It is so deathly dull! We would rather be picking flowers in the gardens of the

Alhambra or riding our horses, but I suppose this is the training that is required for a future queen.

After Señor Columbus shot me the withering glance, I settled down and listened. He has a gift for speaking and he captivated the entire court with his talk of claiming a new land with glory and riches for the kingdom of Spain. Then he laid out his plea for Queen Isabella to supply him with ships and enough gold and men to undertake the journey.

"Columbus," the Queen said. "You are asking me to squander the wealth of my kingdom and risk the lives of my men. Why should I do this?"

"Because you are a great queen," Columbus said, "and because God himself has told me that I shall succeed."

There was a murmur throughout the court and then Tomas de Torquemada, the Chief Inquisitor, stepped forward. He looked as fearsome as ever, dressed in his blood-red robes with his men flanking him on either side.

"Señor Columbus," de Torquemada said, "how can you be sure it is God? Perhaps it is the devil you have been speaking with!"

Columbus looked Tomas de Torquemada in the eye. "I tell you, sir, a miraculous voice came and whispered to me in the night! God will give me the key to the gates of the ocean..."

"Well then he can give you three ships too!" Tomas de Torquemada retorted.

There was laughter from the court, but not from Columbus, or from the Queen. I could see that she was greatly moved by Columbus and convinced by the passion and manner of his speech, but in the end she said, "I am sorry, Columbus. My answer is no."

Columbus bristled, although he bowed politely and said all the right clever words. He left court immediately and as we walked in the gardens that afternoon Joanna and I saw him leaving the city gates, shambling along in his drab brown robes.

"Why does he dress like a monk?" Joanna wondered.

"He's not very dashing, is he?" I agreed. "He hardly looks like an intrepid explorer of the high seas!"

We walked in the gardens for a while then returned to Joanna's chambers and did our embroidery. I am decorating a mantilla of white lace covered in roses and Joanna has been teasing me that I shall wear this for my wedding.

"My wedding to whom?" I laughed.

"Perhaps Philip the Handsome has a companion who would suit you?" she grinned.

"And what is his name?"

"Roberto the Even Handsomer," she said, falling about laughing.

"No!" I was laughing too, "it's Alfonzo the Utterly Devastating!"

We were both laughing so hard we were in tears when the bell rang to signal that we should return to the great hall. The Queen had called her courtiers to her once more.

"I have spent the past hours in discussion with my advisors and in prayer to God," the Queen said, "and I have decided I was too hasty to dismiss Columbus. Three ships are but a small price to pay when his adventures may bring great glory to God and to Spain..."

"Your Majesty," Tomas de Torquemada bowed deeply, "what a pity it is too late! Señor Columbus has left the city for the port of Cadiz. I believe he intends to set sail and enlist the support of the King of France..."

"Then I shall send a rider after him with news of my change of heart before he can depart." Queen Isabella raised herself from her throne. "Fetch me the best rider from my royal guards!"

It was at this moment that Joanna rose to her feet.

"Mama... I mean, my Queen," she corrected herself, then winked at me, "if you really want to catch Columbus you should send Felipa to ride after him. She is the best rider in our kingdom and her Cara Blanca is the fastest horse in your stables."

The court was stunned into silence. All except Tomas de Torquemada.

"Ridiculous," he muttered. "You cannot send the girl."

This was a mistake. For who would dare to tell a woman

who rules the whole of Spain that only a man was fit for any task?

Queen Isabella smiled. "Well, Felipa? Will you do this for me?"

I was trembling and my heart was racing so fast, I had to steady myself as I made a low curtsey.

"Of course, Your Majesty," I said.

"Good," the Queen said. "Then saddle Cara and leave immediately."

As I left the great hall and strode off towards the stables, Joanna ran alongside me with a huge grin on her face.

"Isn't this exciting?" She bounced up and down. "You are off on an adventure!"

"I am off on the open road where I may be attacked by bandits and murdered before I can reach Columbus and Cadiz!" I whispered at her. "What were you thinking, offering my services like that?"

"Oh, Felipa!" Joanna linked her arm through mine as we walked on. "Do not think about the dangers – think only of the fun. You are so lucky that you are not a princess like me. I would never be allowed to go off on my own. And you know I am right – you are a finer horseman than any man in our kingdom. No one else can ride Cara Blanca!"

I blushed at her words. As a young filly Cara was considered a 'Diablo' – a devil horse. Every one of the grooms in the royal stables tried to ride her and all of them had been thrown violently from her back.

Wild and dangerous, they called her. I did not listen to their warnings. I was a slip of a girl, but I climbed onboard her back without fear. To everyone's astonishment, she never once tried to buck or rear. From that moment we belonged together, for no other horse in the kingdom gave me such joy to ride.

In the stables that day I bade Joanna farewell and saddled Cara on my own. I led her out to the courtyard where the Queen's guard waited for me with a letter to Columbus, composed in Her Majesty's own hand and closed with the royal seal. I took this from him, along with a bag of gold maravedis, mounted up and waited for the guards to raise the portcullis, riding out beneath it and heading to the south towards the port of Cadiz.

I had to hold Cara in check as we set off. She is such a spirited horse. She was prancing about, head held high. Her blue eyes had fire in them, as if she knew that we were riding out at the bidding of the Queen.

The roads between Granada and Cadiz were legendary for being rife with bandits. I was a young girl, alone, with no protectors, and if the scoundrels knew that I carried a velvet purse filled with the Queen's own gold, they would kill me as soon as they captured me.

"But first they must catch us, eh, Cara?" I leant down low over the mare's neck and urged her on. At a gallop, no thief could touch us.

And gallop we did, along the road to Cadiz. Cara gave her all, and when she began to falter I spoke to her, urging every stride out of her.

Finally she was at the end of her strength. The sweat had foamed and caked on her neck and her breath came in dreadful rasps. I could not push her on for much longer and I was beginning to worry that I would fail in my task when I rounded the bend and saw a shrouded figure directly ahead of me.

"Señor Columbus!" My cries made him stop in his tracks. I brought forth the letter with the royal seal, waving it at him. "I bring news from Queen Isabella!"

He was more gracious that day than I had ever seen him before. He thanked me many times over for the letter. Then he looked covetously at Cara.

"This is a fine horse that you have," Columbus said. "May I take her to ride back to the Queen?"

I was horrified, but I managed to keep my serene expression. "My horse is tired, señor. I should rest her." I handed him the velvet purse. "There is enough gold here to buy yourself a mule so that you may ride back to the Alhambra."

We walked on together, me leading Cara for a half-mile or so until we reached the roadside inn.

I did not tell the innkeeper who I was, but it must have been clear from my bearing and dress that I was a noble woman. He no doubt thought it was strange that I should be abandoned by the man I had arrived with, who bought a mule from him then carried on alone.

He probably thought it stranger still that I should wish to take care of my horse myself rather than leave her to the care of the inn's grooms, feeding and watering her myself before retiring to my room.

The innkeeper has just come to find me. Knowing that a lady might not wish to venture downstairs, he has brought my dinner up to my room. Now I have a plate of stew and bread to warm me. The innkeeper also told me that he has checked on Cara Blanca and put a blanket on her to keep her warm. She has run so valiantly for me today. She is my most beloved horse, and I will never, ever forsake her...

# The Duchess

The real world had ceased to exist for me. I was utterly lost in the pages of Felipa's diary. Her words, so ancient, written hundreds of years ago, were warm and alive in my hands. The text flowed through me like water and I never hesitated as I translated page after page without stumbling.

It was the scream that shocked me out of Felipa's life and back into my own once more. A high-pitched cry, its sound all the more terrifying because it was not human. The clarion call of a wild horse.

*The Duchess!*

I threw the diary down on the sofa and ran. When I reached the pen Annie was already there wrestling with the mare, hanging on to the end of the lead rope attached to the halter. I watched as the Duchess almost lifted Annie off her feet and reared straight up on her hind legs, the whites of her eyes showing as she pawed the air viciously with her front hooves.

Annie jerked on the rope once more to bring the mare back down.

"Stop it!" I rushed over and began to undo the gate. "You're hurting her!"

Annie ignored my pleas and jerked on the rope once more. This time the mare dropped so that she was on all fours.

"Ain't hurtin' her," Annie grunted as she held on to the mare. "I is tryin' to stop her from hurtin' herself."

As she said this, the scream rang out again. The first time I'd heard it, I had assumed it was the Duchess. But the sound came from deep in the jungle behind the house, and now it was accompanied by pounding hoofbeats.

"De stallion," Annie said, her eyes scanning the jungle warily. "He come for her. He want her back."

The Duchess was looking at the jungle too, her head up high, her nostrils flared and her ears pricked.

When she heard the stallion's call she replied with

a high-pitched whinny of her own, fighting once more to free herself from Annie's grasp.

"Why don't you just let her go?" I said to Annie. "If she wants to be wild, then let her."

Annie shook her head. "De wounds are too deep," she insisted. "If she goes now, dey will get infected. De horse needs time to heal."

The Duchess was still stamping and snorting while Annie gripped on desperately to her halter, trying to keep the mare under control.

Annie looked at me, her dark eyes shining. "Here, child. You come and hold her."

I felt my heart pounding. "No! I can't…"

"Child!" Annie's voice was gruff. "Take her from me. I need to get de runes and do a circle."

There was something about the way that Annie barked her orders that made it impossible to refuse. I unhooked the gate to the pen and stepped inside.

"Take hold!" Annie directed.

I reached out and took hold of the halter with both hands as Annie let go.

"Stay dere!"

Annie ran faster than I would have expected an old woman to move, disappearing round the corner of the house.

Suddenly, I was alone with the Duchess. The last time we had been together like this we were waist-deep in mud. Now that we were side by side on dry land I could see just how big the mare was. She was tall, and solid too, with a broad back and powerful neck muscles. She looked strong enough that one good shake of her head would be all it would take to loosen the grip of my feeble hands.

"Good girl, Duchess," I breathed, trying to keep my nerve and hang on.

I could hear the stallion, rustling and stamping his way through the undergrowth of the jungle. Now for a third time he gave his mighty cry, beckoning the mare to him.

The Duchess raised her head, her eerie blue eyes searching the dark jungle that surrounded us.

"You can't go yet," I told her firmly. "You need to stay here until the cuts heal."

Instinctively, I let go of the rope with one hand so that I could stroke her face, and as I did this her blue eyes seemed to lose some of their fire. She acknowledged my touch with a gentle nicker.

Did she recognise me from our ordeal on the mudflats yesterday? Was it possible that she knew that I had tried to save her life?

As if in answer to my question, the Duchess lowered her head and placed her muzzle right up against the back of my hand, almost like a knight kissing a maiden's wrist. I felt her soft lips brush my skin like velvet.

"You got de obeah all right."

Annie had appeared out of nowhere. She was standing outside the pen holding a string of bones and a big bunch of purple herbs. The way she stared at me and the Duchess totally gave me the creeps.

She stood as still as a statue, and then shook herself and began to make this weird clucking noise with her tongue. She had a spooky look on her face and her eyes were rolling back in her head.

"Are you OK?" I asked.

Annie didn't answer. She was shaking the bunch of purple herbs all around herself. She began to walk towards me, shaking the purple herbs around me and around the Duchess and then she beckoned for me to come out of the pen and she thrust the herbs into my hand.

"I... hey... What are you doing?" I asked.

"You gots de obeah. You have to make de magic circle," Annie said. "Make it good and strong, keep de stallion away."

I held the herbs reluctantly – keeping them at arm's length.

"Make de circle," Annie made a sweeping gesture. "Like dis…"

She traced where the circle needed to go, arcing a perimeter all the way round the pen.

"Now, you do it!"

I felt really stupid but I did what she told me, dragging the bunch of purple herbs through the dirt. As I did this, Annie muttered away and jangled a string of chicken bones in her left hand as if they were rosary beads.

"What are those for?"

"Shush, child!" Annie raised the bone hand to silence me. "I is workin'!"

With a few vigorous shakes, she finished her ritual and then took the herbs from me and hung them with the bones on the post near the gate of the pen.

"She be safe," Annie said confidently. "Ain't no way de stallion will get to her now."

Weirdly enough, the sound of hooves was indeed gone. Then again, I figured, this could have just been a coincidence. I failed to see how a bunch of herbs and some bones could drive away a horse. I looked at the Duchess, standing calmly in her pen.

"What will you do with her?" I asked.

"Keep her another day or t'ree," Annie said. "Until de flesh heals on the wounds and she ain't infected. Den I take her back across the island to her home, let her loose again with de herd."

Annie turned to me. I thought she was going to say something important, but then she seemed to change her mind.

"Bee-a-trizz," she shoved her straw hat down firmly over her dreadlocks, "get your things, child. Annie gonna take you home."

I walked back towards the house, still feeling a little wobbly on my legs. I wasn't sure if I had fully recovered from my heatstroke, but I wasn't about to say anything to Annie in case she changed her mind.

I found my backpack hanging on the hook of the front door. I hadn't noticed before now that Annie had rescued it. She must have found it on the beach when she dragged me from the mud hole. It was a little battered, but even my drink bottle was still inside.

I strapped it on and picked up the ancient diary. I held it with reverent care, tracing my finger over the worn gold letters on the cracked leather cover.

It seemed so incredible to be holding a piece of history in my hands. I mean, that had to be *the*

Christopher Columbus she was talking about, right? The date of the diary entry made sense – I remembered the rhyme from school: *In 1492, Columbus sailed the ocean blue.* Felipa's diary was over five hundred years old!

"Take it wit' you."

I looked up to see Annie standing in the doorway. "What?"

Annie gestured at the book in my hands. "Take de diary."

"Really?" I hesitated. "It's very old. It might be valuable…"

Annie laughed. "Child! Take a look around you! Everytink here is old – including me!"

She took the diary from my hands and wrapped it back up in its old dirty rags and shoved it into my backpack.

"You take it, Bee-a-trizz," she insisted. "You be de guardian of de words now."

"But…" I tried to protest but Annie shushed me. "Don't back-sass me, child! Take de book!"

As we left Annie's cottage, I felt relief to be heading home at last, but all the same I worried about leaving the Duchess behind.

Annie seemed convinced that the mare was safe,

because I had drawn a circle in the dirt with a bunch of herbs. But what if the stallion came back while we were gone?

"Is he the herd leader?" I asked Annie as we bumped along. I had to shout to make my voice heard above the tractor engine.

"Who?" Annie shouted back.

"The stallion."

Annie kept her eyes on the track up ahead.

"Mercy no, child!" she laughed. "He ain't de leader. She be de one in charge."

"You mean the Duchess?"

Annie nodded. "Medicine Hat is de boss lady. She one special horse."

"Where is her herd?" I asked.

Annie shrugged. "Most often dey down by de Bonefish Marshes, but dey goes where dey please. Could be anywhere."

"So nobody owns them?"

"No, child," Annie said. "Dey is wild, like I tell you."

"But how did they get here?"

"Nobody knows, child."

"Well they must have been owned by someone once. How did they—"

Suddenly Annie steered the tractor down a steep track where the ground dropped away to one side and I found myself fighting to hang on. I gave up talking after that and clung on to the wheel arch. Later, I wondered if Annie had driven down the bank on purpose just to shut me up.

As it was, I was feeling pretty weak – and it took all my strength just to hang on until we reached the beach and I could see the *Phaedra* anchored in the bay.

I never got the chance to say goodbye to Annie. What with Mom fussing over me, she was gone before I knew it. I never said thank you for the diary either. Was she right that I possessed some strange connection to the ancient book? All I knew was from the moment I held the diary, I couldn't wait for my chance to disappear into its pages once more.

# F.M.

## 10th September, 1493

My heart was singing as we rode back through the gates of the city of the Alhambra. How wonderful to be home at last!

For many months our grand tour has taken the royal court across the whole of Spain. In every village there have been fiestas in the streets. The people of Spain gather and throw garlands of flowers and cry out, "Long Live the Queen!"

Her Majesty always leads the procession for she is an excellent rider. Her stallion Angelus is a difficult creature, always fretting and stamping his impatience to be on the move, but she handles him with such ease. She talks to him as if he is a naughty child, until his temper calms.

Joanna and I always ride directly behind her. Joanna has

several horses but she usually rides Victorioso, a palomino with a very showy golden coat and silver mane. Victorioso is very beautiful but never in a million years would I trade him for my Cara.

Cara Blanca – white face. So pure, like an angel with startling blue eyes. She has a brown marking like a sombrero over her ears and patches of brown on her rump, shoulders and chest too. These make her very special. It was the Queen herself who told me this.

"Do you understand the meaning of her markings?" The Queen asked me one day as we were journeying. She pointed first to Cara's ears. "This holds wisdom," she said. Then she pointed to the dark brown patch that could be seen on Cara's chest. "And this is a shield across her heart," Queen Isabella said. "The sign of the protector."

As we rode through the gates of the Alhambra, Cara seemed to know that we were home. She arched her neck and held her tail high and proud.

"Wave to the crowd!" Joanna told me.

"But I am not a princess!" I replied. "It is you that they wish to see, not me."

"All the same," Joanna said, "you must wave. It makes the people happy."

I did as Joanna told me. I waved until my hand hurt, and then once we were safely inside the palace walls I dismounted from Cara and took the reins of Joanna's palomino too.

"Allow me to put Victorioso away," I said.

"We have stable hands for that," Joanna said.

"But I would rather look after the horses myself," I insisted.

Joanna shrugged. "As you wish, but come back to my chambers straight away. I would like to discuss my clothes – I'm not certain which dress to wear at court tomorrow."

I hesitated. "Oh... The thing is..."

"What?" Joanna frowned.

"I was hoping that I might spend the night at my own home," I said nervously.

My parents have a house in Granada, not far from the palace – I had not seen them in months and I was desperate to see Mama.

"I need you to stay with me," Joanna said. "I cannot dress myself."

"But Joanna..."

I saw the sneer on her face. "Your Royal Highness," I corrected myself. "I promise I will lay out your garments for dinner tonight before I leave for home and I will make sure I am back early in the morning to dress you."

Joanna looked upset. "Do I really have to command you to stay with me? Aren't you my best friend?"

"No!" I said. "I mean, yes, I am your best friend. And I do

want to stay. But I have not seen Mama and Papa in months. Please... it is just for one night..."

Joanna hesitated. Then she waved her hand dismissively at me.

"Go home," she said. "Give my greetings to your family, and do not fail to be back first thing to dress me for breakfast."

"Thank you, Princess!"

After I settled Cara and Victorioso into their familiar stalls I hurried to the royal chambers and laid out Princess Joanna's wardrobe for tonight's dinner. Then I set off on foot, making the short walk to my home.

My parents did not know that the royal party had returned and when my mother opened the door and saw me on the stoop she let out a squeal and flung her arms round me tightly.

"Felipa! My darling!" She held me out at arm's length to examine me. "Look at you! How big you have grown! Oh, and your beautiful new gown!"

"It was a gift from Princess Joanna," I told her proudly.

I must admit after so long in royal company I had grown accustomed to such trappings of luxury. That evening when my father returned home and Mama gaily placed the platters of rice and stewed lamb on the table, I couldn't help but be disappointed. At the palace our meals were always sumptuous banquets, with several courses, and there were always entertainments and servants to do the cleaning up for us.

It was not that my household was poor. My mother had once been the Queen's own companion and she was her distant cousin too. I had noble blood in my veins on Mama's side and my father, a Jew by birth, had converted to the Catholic faith to please the Queen and earn a respected position as the collector of taxes in Granada.

Mama was busy asking me questions.

"Tell me about the fashions in Barcelona!" she said. "What are the ladies wearing?"

"Never mind such trifling matters!" my father said. "They say that there is plague in that city."

"It is so horrible," I told them. "The plague strikes down commoners and nobles alike. First comes the fever and delirium, and very soon afterwards great black pustules appear and then the very blood inside the body appears to boil and spew forth..."

"Felipa!" My mother had turned quite pale. "Please! Not while we are eating dinner!"

"Sorry, Mama," I said. "I am only repeating what I have heard. When news of the plague reached the court the Queen's advisors insisted that we must leave immediately. We rode straight back to Granada in just three days."

My father wanted to know more, but Mama diverted the

subject to the goings-on at court. "I hear that Christopher Columbus made his triumphant return and travelled to Barcelona for an audience with the Queen," she said. "Did he remember you?"

"If he knew me, he did not show it," I said. "He thinks he is quite grand now that the Queen has made him her Admiral of the High Seas. He turned up at court dressed in a velvet hat and cape and his men stood beside him with gifts of brilliantly coloured parrots, and animals, and most amazing of all – six Indians, natives of the land he had discovered."

"And what did these natives look like?" my mama asked with wide eyes.

"They were quite savage," I told her. "Dressed in no more than paint and feathers, naked and shivering. I heard that one of them had already died of the cold when they arrived. The Queen has taken the remaining six into her care. She is teaching them her faith so that they can become good Catholics."

"It sounds like they need warm clothes, not the words of God," my father said.

My mother's face turned anxious and she pushed her dinner aside.

"Is something wrong, Mama?" I asked.

"No, Felipa," my mother insisted. "It is just that it has been a year since the Queen made her ruling that the Jews are to leave Spain. Many of our friends were forced to abandon their homes and possessions and all that they hold dear..."

My father interrupted her. "I have told your mother that the royal decree does not apply to us. We are dear friends of the Queen and we are Conversos – we now live in the Catholic faith."

I agreed with my father. "The Queen is always very sweet and generous to me, even though she knows I have Jewish blood in my veins."

"All the same," my mother persisted. "They say Tomas de Torquemada sends his men to drag decent families from their homes..."

"As if Torquemada and his inquisitors would dare to question the Queen's own tax collector!" my father scoffed. "We are under Her Majesty's protection. You will see."

My mother did not argue again. She began to clear away the dinner plates from the table.

I went to my room and later, when my mother came upstairs with a basket of laundry, I noticed that she had a red welt on her wrist. "There was a flea," she said, "when I unpacked your clothes from Barcelona. It must have bitten me."

# F.M.

## 17th September, 1493

The Princess was in a cheerful mood when I returned to her. She seemed to have forgotten her outburst of the day before.

"It is a lovely day!" she said. "We should saddle up and go for a ride together after breakfast."

We left the palace gates and were cantering through the countryside when I saw a farmer bent down low over a dark shape in a field not far away from us.

"What is he doing?" Joanna wondered, and with her usual impetuousness she rode straight towards him.

When we were closer I saw that he knelt over a newborn foal. It was jet black, and very beautiful, but to look upon it broke my heart as it was dead. The man had clearly killed it with his own hands, but now he sat weeping over the lifeless body.

"Why did you do this?" I asked him, choking back tears.

The farmer looked up at me. "I had no choice," he said. "The Church has decreed that all black horses are the servants of Satan. If a black foal is born then it must not be allowed to live."

"This cannot be true," I said. "Surely a horse cannot be judged by the colour of its coat to be good or evil?" I found it hard to believe that the Church considered black horses cursed.

I looked at the poor foal lying dead in the dust and something inside me snapped. "This is Tomas de Torquemada's work," I said to Joanna. "He is a madman! We have to do something!"

I expected Joanna to agree with me. She loves horses just as much as I do. But instead she pulled her lips taut.

"My mother appointed Tomas de Torquemada to be the hand of God. Do you question the will of the Queen?"

We rode back to the Alhambra in silence. In my mind I kept seeing the black foal, its eyes glassy in death, and I thanked God for Cara with her special markings, the brown sombrero over her ears and the shield at her chest… the markings of good fortune and protection.

I took both horses to the stables and I spent a long time

brushing Cara, mostly to avoid seeing any more of Joanna until I had to. I felt uneasy in her company right now.

Cara stood with her usual regal bearing while I groomed her silken mane and sang to her. Then I mixed her feed, and put a bale of alfalfa in her hay rack before dusting myself off and heading to the royal chambers to prepare the Princess for court.

The Queen's return to the Alhambra had created an air of excitement. All afternoon a steady parade of noblemen arrived at the palace seeking an audience with Her Majesty. The Queen sat on her throne and listened intently as they took their turn to step forward to ask her favours.

When Tomas de Torquemada spoke he gave a report on the Inquisition. He delighted in a story about a Converso who turned out to be a secret Jew and had betrayed the Queen.

The Queen listened and nodded in solemn agreement as Tomas told her that the man had been sentenced to be burnt alive.

The business of court had almost drawn to a close when Christopher Columbus entered the room.

He strode proudly up the great hall and as he took his bow he gave a ridiculous flourish of his hat so that the plume almost poked his nose. I did not dare look at Joanna as I'm sure she would have reduced me to fits of giggles.

"Admiral Columbus," the Queen said. "Your men are prepared to sail?"

"We have seventeen ships ready to depart," Columbus agreed.

"Excellent," the Queen said. "Then allow me to make a gift to you."

The Queen gestured to her guards and with trumpets blowing a fanfare the doors of the great chamber of the Alhambra were opened and the strangest procession was brought forth. There were cows yoked together and goats too, trotting and bleating their way into the middle of the Queen's court. I heard Lady Margritte shriek as a pig trampled her skirts.

"My gifts to you, Admiral Columbus," the Queen said, sweeping an arm before the carts filled with chickens, geese, ducks and rabbits. "Take them on this journey so that you may have everything you need to establish a new colony for Spain."

Admiral Columbus looked pleased. "Your Majesty is generous and kind," he said. And then he hesitated. "But there is one more animal I require. I shall need horses. At least a dozen for myself and my men. Six stallions to ride and six mares to breed from."

"Of course," the Queen said. "Twelve horses shall be yours."

\*\*\*

"Those poor horses!" I said to Joanna. "How dreadful to be taken by Columbus and kept cramped up onboard his ship for months on end..."

Joanna didn't reply. She lay on her bed and watched as I put out her gown for dinner.

"There!" I said brightly. "Now I will be back first thing in the morning to prepare you for breakfast."

I was about to leave when Joanna spoke. Her voice was tinged with bitterness.

"Do not think you can keep abandoning me like this without consequences," she said.

I hesitated in the doorway, then replied, "Of course, my Princess," and closed the door behind me.

It was late evening by the time I reached my parents' house. "Mama? Papa?" I cried out as I came through the door. "I have news! Admiral Columbus has returned..."

My father came downstairs in haste to meet me. His brow was furrowed with concern.

"Your mother is ill," he said. "She has a high fever and pains all over."

I was shocked as my mother never took ill. "I will take up a damp compress to soothe her," I said and went to climb the stairs, but my father blocked my path.

"Your mother insisted that I do not let you see her, for fear her infection may spread."

"But she needs me! She is ill!"

"Leave her be," my father said. "Tomorrow the fever will have broken and you may visit her bedside."

There was no one to cook my dinner that night – so I had a humble meal of soup and bread. I am putting my diary aside – it has been a very long day and I need to sleep.

# The Obeah

When I am lost in the pages of Felipa's diary, I imagine that I am her. It must have been amazing to live back then – to be best friends with a princess and to ride horses all day. Instead, I am stuck on a boat with a mother who is totally unreasonable.

"You know there have to be consequences, Beatriz," Mom said, coming into my room later that evening. "You can't just wander off by yourself, without telling me where you're going."

"Mom… stop making a big deal—"

"You disappeared!" Mom snapped. "You were gone for nearly two days and you didn't call."

"Because my phone was dead."

"Anything could have happened to you!"

How much more furious she would be if she found out about the mud hole!

Finally Mom delivered her punishment. "I think you'd better stay on the *Phaedra* tomorrow," she said.

"Am I grounded?" I asked.

"You're not exactly on the ground," my mom mused. "It might be more accurate to say you are watered."

"That's not funny."

"Neither is wandering off on your own halfway across the island and spending the night on some crazy woman's sofa."

That night all I wanted was to disappear into Felipa's diary again. But I couldn't read it with Mom in the room. I didn't want her to ask questions about where I had got it from.

I was exhausted and I guess I fell straight asleep. When I woke up it was morning and my first thought was of the Duchess. I knew that Annie would be looking after her, but all the same I felt bad about leaving her there. I just had this feeling like it was my job to make sure she was OK, like I should have stayed with her.

When I came up on deck Mom was at the bow of the *Phaedra*. She had her binoculars trained on a cluster of rocks near the mouth of the bay.

"Here, take a look," she said, passing them to me.

I held the binoculars to my face and looked in the direction she was pointing.

"I can't see anything."

"Keep looking," Mom told me. "A little to the left…"

Suddenly a sleek flash of silver broke the surface of the water, rising up in an arc into the sky and then splashing back down.

"What is it?" I asked. "A dolphin?"

Mom shook her head. "It's a swordfish," she said. "It looks like it's on the hunt. There must be jellyfish over there, maybe sea thimbles."

Jellyfish are like French fries to a swordfish – virtually their favourite food.

"I'm taking the Zodiac to go and look," Mom said.

She was already strapping on her life jacket. I stood on the deck and looked out through the binoculars again and saw the swordfish perform a spectacular leap, rising right out of the water so that its tail seemed to flip it into the air. Its nose really was like a sword, a blade cutting into the water as it dived.

"Beatriz?"

"Hmmph?"

"I said are you coming?"

I shook my head. "No."

If you want to know the truth, I would've liked to have seen the swordfish up close, but I was being difficult I guess. After all, Mom never came to see the hoofprints. It is always about what she wants to do and never what I want.

Mom was already climbing down the ladder and untying the ropes on the inflatable.

"Do your homework while I'm gone," she told me as she started the outboard motor. I watched her roar off across the waves, heading out towards the rocks, and then I went to the kitchen where Mom's laptop was already open on the table.

I was about to open my school folder on the desktop when I noticed an email in Mom's inbox. It was from my dad. The subject line simply said *Re: Beatriz.*

I hesitated and then I moved the arrow on to the email and felt my tummy tie in a knot as I took a deep breath and gave it a click.

Maria,

You are being totally unreasonable. I can only imagine what you've told Beatriz. I am sure that you have no hesitation in painting me as the bad guy, but let's not forget you are the one who packed your bags and left with her. Don't try to make it look like you are always in the right. Sometimes you have to listen to me. And don't bother to reply to this. When you have calmed down then maybe we can talk.

    Rob

I read the email twice. I nearly deleted it by mistake because my hands were shaking so much.

I took a deep breath – then I typed out a message and left it on the screen right beside the email from my dad.

"Gone out – back soon," it said. This time Mom couldn't complain that I hadn't left a note.

I swam in my clothes and my reef boots. I figured they would dry out soon enough – the sun was so hot. I was in the water and about halfway to shore when I paused and looked back across the sea at Mom in the Zodiac. She was staring out through her binoculars at the horizon. She could be there for hours. She wouldn't even notice

I was gone. I put my head down and began to swim harder.

I didn't think Annie was crazy like Mom said, but she sure was strange. The truth was the thought of going back to her house creeped me out, but I couldn't just leave the Duchess there. I had to go back and make sure my horse was OK.

Those rickety pens at Annie's house wouldn't hold up if the stallion came back. Annie seemed to have a lot of faith in the power of a magic circle, but I wasn't so sure that stallion was the sort to be scared off by a bunch of purple herbs.

I got my bearings, taking the same path as before into the jungle. When I reached that massive old tree in the clearing I got the same prickly feeling down my spine. I stood there for a moment in silence, and I felt sort of like I was paying my respects to the tree before I could move on. Then I kept walking, cutting a path through the jungle, all the way to the mudflats.

I crossed the mudflats carefully, making sure to stay well clear of the hole, keeping to the areas where the marsh grass was firm underfoot, all the way across to the hills where the jungle rose up before me and deep gouged tyre tracks led me to Annie's little yellow cottage.

The bottles were tinkling in the tree like wind chimes when I arrived. It gave me a shiver as I walked past. I think all of Annie's talk about obeah was starting to get to me.

Annie was in the pens at the back of the cottage. And there was my beautiful horse again.

"Bee-a-trizz," she said without turning round to face me, "hand me that halter, will you, child?"

Did she have eyes in the back of her head? The way she spoke to me was odd too, like as far as she was concerned I had never been gone.

I stepped forward and handed her the halter. She took it from me with a grunt, still keeping her back to me. On the fence post alongside her there was a big tub of gooey green paste that Annie had been using on the Duchess's hindquarters. The rope marks had already healed a little in just one day.

"She looks a lot better," I said.

Annie gave the Duchess a pat on her rump. "She a strong spirit. She heal fast. Another day, maybe two and I take her back to de herd."

"Will you ride her back?" I asked.

Annie looked at me as if I was the crazy one. "Mercy no, child! I tell you de mare is a Medicine

Hat. She got de strong obeah. Ain't nobody can ride a Medicine Hat unless dey is chosen."

"So who chooses you?"

Annie laughed. "De horse, child, who else? De horse chooses de rider."

Annie peered at me with her black eyes shining. "You see de markings, Bee-a-trizz?" she asked, pointing at the brown patch over the Duchess's chest. "De mark of de protector. You get chosen to ride a Medicine Hat and ain't notink can hurt you."

Crazy old lady. That's what my mom would have said. But I didn't think Annie was crazy. *The mark of the protector.* That was the same thing Queen Isabella had said about Cara!

"Annie?"

"Yes, child?"

"A Medicine Hat – those markings are pretty rare, right?"

Annie grunted. "Very special, de rarest kind."

I looked at the Duchess. Her blue eyes held my stare.

"What is it, child?" Annie looked at me. "Tell Annie what you thinkin'."

I took a deep breath. "That day, when you got

me out of the mud and you brought me here? I had a fever and I... I had this weird dream."

Annie's hands suddenly stilled and she nodded for me to continue.

"Well, not like a dream exactly..." I said. "I can't explain, but it felt real – like it was actually happening. And there was a horse. And the thing is, she looked just like the Duchess, with the same markings on her ears and the shield on her chest. *The mark of the protector.*"

Annie took a deep breath and let out a low whistle. "Didn't I told you, Bee-a-trizz?" she said. "You is got de obeah. It give you sight. Make you special."

Annie didn't think I was daydreaming or lying. She knew I was telling the truth.

"And I think it's connected to the diary," I continued breathlessly, "the one you gave me? I've been reading it and there's a horse. Her name is Cara Blanca and she has markings just like the Duchess too..."

"You been readin' the old diary?" Annie asked.

I nodded.

"Good, good," Annie grunted. "You be de guardian of de words, Bee-a-trizz. You take care of dem."

I shook my head. "You know, I really think the diary must be valuable. Like an antique or something. You should have it back."

Annie frowned. "It ain't mine, child. If you be goin' to give it back, best you give it to de tree."

*Give it to the tree.* It was a weird thing to say, even by Annie's standards.

"Do you mean because paper comes from trees?" I asked.

Annie shook her head and gave a laugh. "You see. Annie take you home soon and on de way I show you…"

We didn't leave straight away. Annie got me to help out with the Duchess first. I put more potion on her cuts and mixed her feed and filled the trough with water, scoop by scoop. I watched the mare take big deep gulps and then play with the leftovers in the tub, flicking her nose back and forth. The way she was around me, she didn't seem at all wild. There was a calm about her. She even let me stroke her and put braids in her mane. I could have spent hours there, just being with my special horse.

While I was grooming the Duchess, Annie carried on with her yard work, feeding the chickens and weeding out the gardens. She went inside for a while and I could hear her in the kitchen chopping vegetables and rattling pots. Then she emerged from the front door with her straw hat pushed down over her dreadlocks.

"Let's go, Bee-a-trizz!"

She drove the tractor back the same way we had gone yesterday, with me perched up behind on the wheel arch. The ride was just as bumpy as last time, but my arms could handle it better now that I wasn't so sick and exhausted.

When we drove through the snakewood and pigeon berry and entered the clearing by the big tree, Annie pulled the tractor to a stop and cut the engine.

"We be arrived," she said.

I felt the hairs on the back of my neck stand up. She'd driven us straight back to the clearing in the jungle.

Annie walked over to the tree and caressed the trunk as if it was made of velvet, and when she turned back to me her black eyes were glistening.

"Dis be a Jumbie tree," she said. "Very old. Full of ghosts."

She was starting to creep me out again. I stayed where I was on the wheel arch and didn't move a muscle. The jungle around us had gone strangely quiet. The parrots were silent and there was a powerful stillness to the air.

"Come here, child," Annie beckoned. "Come see…"

I didn't move.

"Listen," Annie insisted. "The ghosts be callin' you. You can hear them, child. Come closer…"

I didn't hear them, but I sure could feel something. I was shivering all over as I steeled myself and slid down from the tractor. I walked slowly over to where Annie stood at the base of the tree.

"Now look up," Annie said. "Do you see it, Bee-a-trizz? Just above your head? Here, let me lift you and you can look."

She grasped me round the waist and raised me up off my feet.

In the trunk of the tree, too far up for me to see it on my own, there was a hole. It must have started out as a knot in the wood, but it had been chiselled away and hollowed out so that there was a cavity inside the trunk, a hole about the size of my head. It had been made a long time ago, but I could still see the cuts and the grooves in the bark. I stared inside. It was empty.

Annie lowered me back down.

"Dat is where I found de diary," she told me. "So you see, Bee-a-trizz, if you want to give it back, you don't give it to me. You give it to de tree."

\*\*\*

Mom was waiting for me on the *Phaedra* when I swam back. She didn't even give me a chance to dry off before she launched into my telling-off.

"Are you determined to make me mad? Is that your plan?" she asked.

"I wasn't doing it to annoy you," I insisted. "I had to go and see Annie – she has my horse."

Mom looked stunned. "Beatriz, I told you specifically that you weren't allowed to go back there again. And the first thing you do is disobey me?"

"You're always telling me what to do," I snapped. "I'm old enough to make my own mind up about stuff."

"You're twelve, Beatriz, and as long as I am looking after you I get to make the decisions about what is best," Mom said.

"It's my life and I get to decide too," I shot back. "If I want to go and live with Dad in Florida you have to let me."

"No," Mom said. "I don't. You live here with me, Beatriz. That's the way it is and that's final. And by the way you aren't allowed to look at my emails without asking. It's terribly rude."

"So you get to make all the rules and I don't even get a say?"

"Oh please, Beatriz! You act like I'm being unreasonable when you're the one who has run off to that crazy old island woman and… Beatriz! Don't walk away from me…"

But I didn't want to listen. I stomped downstairs, shut the door behind me and threw myself on my bunk.

I expected Mom to come after me, but she didn't. I lay there for a while, listening to my heart pounding. I hate Mom sometimes!

Then I dug around in the drawer beneath my bed, took out the diary marked with Felipa's golden initials and I began to read.

# F.M.

## 18th September, 1493

In the middle of the night I was woken by screams. At first I thought I'd been having nightmares, but then I realised the cries were quite real. They were coming from upstairs.

"Mama!"

I raced to the top of the landing and as I reached Mama's bedroom Papa flung open the door.

"No, Felipa," he pleaded. "Stay back! You can't help her – it is too dangerous."

I looked over his shoulder and caught sight of my mother lying on the bed. Her body looked so frail, bed clothes soaked with sweat, her hands outstretched, eyes bulging with terror.

"Felipa!" she called out. "My dear sweet Felipa…"

"No!" My father put his arms across the doorway and barred my path. "No, Felipa! Do not go near her. You must get away from this place. Leave this house now — do you hear me?"

"Let me through!" I was screaming. "I want to see Mama!"

I tried to fight my way past but Papa shoved me roughly away before slamming the door shut and bolting it from the inside.

Outside the bedroom, I clawed desperately at the handle.

"Mama!" I cried. "Let me in! What is happening?"

But in my heart I knew. In that brief glimpse of my mama I had seen the black swellings on the side of her throat and the ruby-red flush of her cheeks, hot with fever. I knew why my father would not let me in. He was trying to save my life. Mama had the black plague.

I pressed myself up to the door listening in horror to my mother's wails on the other side.

"Mama," I sobbed. "Mama, I am here. I am here."

The black plague is a brutal death, and, in my mother's case, it was mercifully swift. Very soon her screams became pitiful whimpers and moans, and then these too grew weaker until they ceased altogether.

I slumped down and cried her name again and again. I knew there was nothing I could do. By the time the dawn's clear light broke it was over. Mama was dead.

"May I see her?" I begged my father when he opened the door at last. "Please, Papa?"

My father shook his head.

"Even in death she may pass the sickness on to you," he said.

I never looked upon my mother's face again. Papa held me back as they took her from the house wrapped in the bedsheets. Everyone was so afraid the plague might infect them – even the priest would not come to our house. For Mama to die without God's pardon was a dreadful thing. This was the cruel, final curse of the plague. No last rites and no funeral.

My stomach felt sick as I watched them throw her, as if she was no more than a sack of spoiled corn, on to a dump cart.

"Where are they taking her?" I asked.

"To the outskirts of the city," my father said. "To be put upon a pyre and burned."

I stood in the street and watched them loading Mama's possessions on to the cart alongside her. Her clothes and finery, all to be burnt in case they too carried the plague. Nothing of hers remained. I had not so much as a keepsake to remember her by.

My father was not an affectionate man. He had no words of comfort for me as we watched her being driven away, so when he turned to go back inside I could not bring myself to follow. Only death and emptiness lay there. I turned and ran. I had to flee from the horrors I had just witnessed.

I raced through the narrow cobbled streets towards the Alhambra. It was late afternoon and the streets were deserted – it was too hot to be outdoors. The sun burned and my lungs felt like they would burst. Still I kept running, all the way through the orange trees and the fountains until I had reached the royal stables.

My feet had taken me where my heart needed to go, and I found myself padding down the corridor towards Cara's stall.

"Cara?" I unbolted the door, my hands trembling, and at the sound of my voice she began to nicker, calling to me in the gloom.

"Oh, Cara!" I flung my arms round her neck, holding on to her desperately, feeling the tears come in great floods. I buried my face deep into her mane and felt as miserable as I had ever been in my whole life.

I cried for Mama, sobbing my heart out until my eyes were puffy and swollen and my head throbbed. My fingers tangled in Cara's mane as I clung to my horse taking comfort from her, taking strength from her strength.

When at last I had worn myself out and had collapsed into the straw bedding on the stable floor, Cara did the most remarkable thing. She came over to me and, nickering softly, she snuffled me with her muzzle, as if trying to rouse me.

Then, when she could see that I was too weak to stand, she dropped to her knees and lay alongside me, so that I was able to put my arms round her. I held on tight, feeling her heart beating against my own as I curled up against the brown marking on her chest – the sign of the protector.

I was exhausted, but I could not fall asleep. Every time I shut my eyes I could see the eyes of my mother staring at me, so terrified as the plague took its grip. Her anguished cries rang in my ears.

I clung to Cara and gathered what remained of my strength, and then I stood up and left the stables and headed for home.

My father would be waiting for me. With my mother gone, he was all the family that I had. The thought that I had been trying to banish from my head became ever more real as I neared the house. Father had been with Mama when she was dying. What if he too had caught the plague? What if he already had begun to feel its gruesome effects?

When I reached our house my fears grew worse. The front door was hanging wide open.

"Father?" I walked inside and called for him but there was no reply.

"Father!" I raced up the stairs, expecting to find him in the bedroom, prepared for the worst. But when I reached the room there was no one there. The house was empty. My father was gone.

I felt completely bewildered. The house, which had been wracked with moans and pitiful cries, was now silent. I went and checked in my father's wardrobe. His clothes and his travelling bag were all still there.

I waited for a while, thinking he would return. After all, where else would he go? I even began to prepare for him, tidying the kitchen and baking bread in case he was hungry. Kneading the dough kept my hands busy and eased my fears, but by the time the loaf had cooled he had still not returned.

I was certain something was very wrong. I left the bread uneaten and headed out of the house. I had to see the one person who might be able to help me to find my father.

\*\*\*

"Mom?" I was sitting at the table watching her cook dinner. "What's the black plague?"

"A disease carried by rats," Mom said. "The rats were infested with fleas and if the fleas bit you then you got the plague."

"And then you died?"

"Pretty much," Mom said. "It killed millions of people hundreds of years ago. Whole towns and cities were infected."

"Can you still get it now?"

Mom shook her head. "Not in the Bahamas, sweetie."

"That's good," I said, "because I wouldn't want you to die from it."

Mom looked at me like I was talking crazy. "Thanks for your concern, Bee."

"So, umm, there's no plague in Florida either?"

Mom stopped stirring the paella.

"Bee? You need to let go of this idea of moving back with your Dad, OK? He's just not in a good place right now."

I was going to say something smart, like, "I thought he was in Florida," but I didn't want to get into a fight again. I'd been fighting so much with Mom lately and I hated it.

Also, my only way off this boat was to make peace. And I desperately wanted to get back to the island.

"Did you see how I washed down the decks?" I asked. "And I cleaned the cabin windows too."

Mom raised an eyebrow at me. "OK, Beatriz, what are you angling for?"

"Nothing!" I insisted as she dished up the plates of paella. I sat there and waited for her to join me at the table and then I said, really casually, "Hey, Mom, can I take the Zodiac out tomorrow?"

"I suppose so," Mom said. "Where are you planning on going?"

"Round the coast."

There was a tense pause. I held my breath.

"Wear a life jacket, please," Mom said. "And be back by dinner."

"Sure," I said.

I spent the rest of dinner asking Mom questions about her work so that she wouldn't ask me about what my plans were. I *had* told the truth when I said I was going round the coast. I just hadn't mentioned my final destination, had I?

# F.M.

## 19th September, 1493

My mother's death had kept me from my duties at court. I knew that Princess Joanna would be upset, but surely when she discovered the reason for my absence there would be no need to apologise. Together we could go to the Queen and I could ask her to help me find my father.

Joanna was not in her chambers and so I made my way directly to the grand hall of the Alhambra. There was music playing and voices and laughter inside, but all of it stopped as I walked in.

Ladies turned to face the wall as if the mere act of looking at me would somehow infect them with plague. At least I had thought that it was the plague that they shied away from. I realised later that I was wrong.

The Queen was not present and Joanna was at the far end of the hall, talking with some of the courtiers. I ran to her, feeling hot tears prick my eyes. I was expecting her to embrace me as she always did, but she held herself stiffly. I felt so embarrassed to be denied her affection that I dropped to my knee in a clumsy curtsey instead.

"Dearest Joanna," I said, "I have come to ask your help. I have been away from court because my mother was sick with plague. I watched her die and fled in grief, and now I have just returned home in great distress only to find my father missing..."

I had known Joanna all my life. Since I was old enough to talk we had shared our secrets and our dreams with each other. She was like a sister to me. And until that moment, I had thought I meant the same to her, but when I lifted my face to hers I saw – nothing. No tears, no emotion. No sweetness and no sympathy.

"Felipa, I am sorry to hear news of your mother..." Joanna's voice was cold. "However, the matter of your father is out of my hands. I cannot interfere for not even a princess is above the will of God."

I was stunned. "What are you talking about? Princess Joanna, where is my father?"

It was not the Princess who answered my question. The doors to the grand hall swung open and Tomas de Torquemada strode in, his red-robed guards of the Inquisition flanking him on either side.

"Lady Felipa Molina," he spoke loud enough so that all those assembled in the hall could hear, "your father has been taken to the dungeons."

I looked at him, my heart pounding. "I'm sorry... I do not understand. Why would my father be in the dungeons?"

Tomas de Torquemada held me with his cold eyes, as if weighing up his next move, and when he spoke his words were a knife in my heart.

"Your father allowed your mother to die without last rites. He mocks the one true faith of the Catholic religion. The Inquisition has taken him so that we may see if his heart is true to the Church and to the Queen."

The poison that he spoke! To use my mother's death as an excuse to imprison my father! Oh, Mama, you were right. Tomas de Torquemada had been secretly plotting against our family all along. And, if the Chief Inquisitor had his way, my papa was going to die.

# Island Stallion

It was further to go by sea to get to Annie's crib, but I figured it would take about the same amount of time because I didn't have to do the long walk through the jungle.

I set off early, saying goodbye to Mom at breakfast and getting underway before she changed her mind. I motored the Zodiac south all the way along the coast of the nature reserve to the very end of the island and then back up the other side, along past Saw Mill Sink, until I reached the mudflats. I tried to hug the shoreline most of the way, and I kept the engine going slow, looking out for submerged rocks. The navigation only got tricky when I reached the mudflats. The sea was shallow and I was constantly in danger of beaching the Zodiac on the sandbanks. I steered my way between mangroves, looking for the deep channels where the water was dark turquoise. Eventually the water wasn't deep enough for the motor or even to row so I had to give up and drag the Zodiac on to the sand. I left it behind and trekked the rest of the way to Annie's on foot, lugging my backpack with me. It contained two things – my water bottle and the ancient diary.

Annie was out back hammering bits of wood on to the horse pens. It looked like she was building a wall or something.

As soon as she saw me she put her tools down and gave me a friendly grin. "Bee-a-trizz! Where you been, child?"

"Nowhere," I shrugged. "Just at home."

"You is just in time to help me," Annie said. "I be carryin' de Duchess back to de marshes."

"Is she ready to go back to the herd?" I asked.

"Come see for yourself," Annie said.

The Duchess was tied up away from the pens at the other side of the cottage. When she caught sight of me she called out, raising her head up and doing this high-pitched whinny like she was saying hello.

She looked all pleased to see me with her ears pricked forward. It felt pretty amazing, her greeting me like an old friend.

"She know you, Bee-a-trizz!" Annie looked just as pleased. "For sure, she know you."

The strange thing is, I felt like I knew her too. Not just because of the mud hole. It was more than that. *Like I'd always known her.* Maybe it was Annie's talk about having the obeah that had started me thinking there was something special between me and the Duchess, but I felt it more and more. I walked straight up to her, picked up one of Annie's brushes and began untangling the burrs from her mane. It came so naturally to me, like I'd been caring for this horse all my life.

I don't know what was in Annie's potion, but the wounds from the ropes had totally healed. All that was left were raw marks of bare skin where the fur was yet to grow back. Annie was right – the mare was well enough now to return to the herd.

"You want to carry her wit' me?" Annie asked as she tied a rope to the Duchess's halter and opened up the gate.

I had the job of watching out for the Duchess off the back of the tractor while Annie drove. It was fun for the first half-hour or so and then my arms began to ache.

"You all right back dere, Bee-a-trizz?" Annie shouted over her shoulder.

"Yeah," I said, keeping a white-knuckle grip on the wheel arch.

"We is almost dere," Annie said. "De Bonefish Marshes dey up ahead."

"I can't see any horses," I said.

"You see dem trees?" Annie pointed to the Caribbean pines dotting the shoreline. "Dey be in de trees takin' shelter."

We bumped along for a bit longer and then Annie said, "Your mama she must be a strong woman, Bee-a-trizz. Takin' you out on de sea, all de way from nowhere, just de two of you."

I had never thought about Mom like that. "I guess so," I said reluctantly.

"Where your daddy at?" Annie asked.

"He lives in Florida," I said. "He wants me to go and live with him but Mom won't let me."

"Is that so?" Annie said. She kept driving the tractor, her eyes focused on the path ahead. I could tell by her tone of voice that she didn't believe me.

140

"He does!" I insisted. I could feel my face going redder, my fist closing tighter on the wheel arch. I thought about what Mom had said to me about Dad last night and then I thought about Annie's tree, the one for keeping away the evil, strung with empty bottles.

"Did you drink all the beer in those bottles on your tree?" I asked.

Annie grunted. "Suppose I must have done," she said. "Ain't no one else here to drink dem."

"My dad drinks too," I told her. "Mom says he can't help it. She says he's got a problem."

"Is that so?" Annie said. And this time I could tell she believed me.

The Caribbean pines were tall and skinny enough for Annie to drive between them. She kept on going until we were right inside the jungle but when we reached a clearing in the middle of the trees she slowed down the tractor to a stop.

"Dey is near," she said.

I didn't see any sign of any horses. The Duchess seemed to sense something though, because she began flinging her head around, pulling back on the rope.

"Let her loose now, Bee-a-trizz," Annie said.

I leapt down off the wheel rim. I was trying to undo the knots in the rope halter when the Duchess almost lifted me off my feet, raising her head right up in the air. As she dragged me skywards she whinnied out louder than I had ever heard her cry before. Her call cut through the air, and then, a few heartbeats later, there came the reply. A whinny just as loud and insistent as her own, seeking her out, coming for her.

"Let her loose, Bee-a-trizz!" There was an anxious tone to Annie's voice. "Don't be messin' around."

"I'm trying!" I said. "I can't get the knot out of the halter."

Annie jumped down off the tractor and came to help me. She sure could move fast for an old woman if she wanted to.

"Who done tied this?" she asked as her gnarled fingers worked the knot.

I am pretty good at knots, but I must have used the wrong one on the halter. It should have been a slip knot but it wasn't. And it was impossible to untie. Annie clawed at it in vain with her fingernails.

"Wait here," she said. "Hold on!"

Annie shoved the lead rope back in my hand. I could have just let the Duchess go, but if she was turned loose with her rope halter still on then there was too much risk that she would get it caught up or tangled on a tree. We needed to get the ropes off her before we could set her free.

"Bee-a-trizz!"

Annie thrust her hand towards me and I saw the sharp edge of the metal blade gleaming in the sunlight. "Take it!"

I grasped the handle of the knife and began to saw away at the rope halter. The blade was blunt so the strands severed very slowly. I felt them pinging apart, one by one, until the halter was held together by no more than a few golden strands...

"Bee-a-trizz!" Annie's voice was tense. "Do it now..."

I was about to cut the last threads when the Duchess jerked up her head really hard. The next thing I knew there was a thundering noise and the clearing was suddenly alive with horses.

There were maybe seven or eight of them, but they galloped together, ducking and swerving around the trees, leaping over the uneven ground. I was overawed by their unstoppable power, the terrifying weight of their bodies, the brutal pounding of their legs that reverberated all the way through my body as they shook the ground beneath us.

"Bee-a-trizz!" Annie shouted. "Run to me!"

Annie had climbed up on the tractor and she was frantically waving at me to follow her.

"No!" I shouted back. "I can do this!"

There were only a few more strands to cut through and my horse would be free.

I tried to hold her head steady and saw away at the rope, but the Duchess was flinging herself around in a frenzy. I tried to hang on to her as the horses scattered all around us, diving both sides of the tractor. They all looked the same – dark bay with black manes and tails, matted and dreadlocked with burrs. The biggest horse ran at the rear of the herd. He must have been the stallion – he was massive compared to the rest. He had splashes of white all over, a broad white blaze down his face and a bold Roman nose. As he came close, he didn't peel off like the others, he bore down on me and the Duchess, making straight for us.

"Ho! Ho!"

Annie leapt down off the tractor waving her hands at him. The stallion put his ears flat back in fury, and only swerved at the very last minute. Then he pulled up and wheeled round to face us again. He was poised to attack!

"Get those ropes cut, child, and let her go!" Annie shouted.

"I'm trying!" The Duchess had pulled away from me to the end of the lead rope and I couldn't reach to cut the last strands. She was dragging me forward and I found myself stumbling through the undergrowth as I desperately tried to keep hold.

"Bee-a-trizz!" Annie called out. "Behind you!" I spun round and that was when I saw the stallion bearing down on me. He was running with his neck stretched right out and his lips curled back with teeth bared. I tried to move out of the way, but I had nowhere to go. He rose up on his hind legs and lunged forward but as he struck out, the lead rope behind me went slack. Suddenly the Duchess barrelled past me, knocking me over, and thrust herself between us to fight the stallion.

I fell over backwards, and began to scramble about in the undergrowth, frantically trying to get as far away as I could. I heard a sickening squeal as the Duchess took a blow from the stallion's hooves, and then the two of them went up on their hind legs,

145

limbs locked in a hideous embrace, necks wound together like snakes.

I felt the grasp of strong arms round me and the next thing I knew Annie had dragged me out of harm's way and over to the tractor.

"Duchess!" I shouted.

"Leave her be!" Annie said, hanging on to me. "She can handle herself."

As the stallion dropped back down on all fours, the Duchess seized her chance. She pivoted and aimed a double-barrel kick with both hind legs. She caught the stallion across his shoulders with a powerful blow that knocked him clean over.

The stallion seemed dazed when he got up. He shook out his mane and then trotted off with his head lowered to the edge of the clearing where the rest of the wild herd were standing. They had been watching with ears pricked, waiting for the outcome. The stallion's message was clear. The Duchess had outmanoeuvred him and he admitted defeat.

My courageous horse stood trembling and snorting, noble in victory. Annie picked up the knife and cut the last remaining strands of the rope halter so that it fell from her proud face.

"De Boss lady be back," Annie said as she watched the Duchess canter over and take her place once more in the herd. "And don't nobody be messin' with her."

# F.M.

## 20th September, 1493

When I left the court that day I was stunned, but upon reflection my shock turned to anger. Did Tomas de Torquemada really think he could get away with this? My best friend is the daughter of the Queen! Princess Joanna would help me to save Papa.

"Princess Joanna?" I called for her but she was not in her rooms. I found her instead, already dressed without me in her best gown and roaming the gardens of the Alhambra with two of her handmaidens, picking flowers.

"Your Royal Highness," I curtseyed low. "I have come to ask a great favour. I need you to talk to your mother. Please tell her that my father is a good man; tell her to release him."

Joanna turned to me, her eyes cold.

"Felipa! I will not confront the Queen. It is treason to defy her will and even if I spoke to her, Tomas de Torquemada is the one who has her ear."

"Joanna! How can you not even try to save my father? We are sisters, you and I!"

"You are not my sister," Princess Joanna snapped. "You are my servant – do not forget that."

She paused and then gestured for the handmaidens to leave us.

"Felipa," she said icily, "do not ask me to do what I cannot. If you do not bite your tongue then you will be joining your father in the dungeons. Now hurry to my chambers and fetch my cloak. We are due in court."

It was all I could do to hold my tongue as I sat next to Joanna that afternoon. There were no more smiles or whispers exchanged between us. Even when Admiral Columbus entered the great chamber we did not gossip as we usually did.

Columbus strode up the great hall to stand before the throne. "Your Majesty, I am almost ready to depart the shores of Spain once more. Seventeen ships have been prepared and I have most of my crew and supplies for the voyage."

"Very good, Admiral," the Queen said. "And what of the

horses? You have the twelve that you require to take with you on the voyage?"

"Indeed, Your Majesty," Columbus said. "I have handpicked them myself. If it may please you…"

As he said this, the vast wooden doors at the far end of the chamber opened wide. To the fanfare of trumpets, six of Columbus's men entered, each of them leading a horse by hand.

I think Admiral Columbus delights in making these grand gestures in the hopes of impressing the Queen. The stallions looked magnificent as they made their way down the centre of the hall, their hooves chiming out against the stone cobbles. Three were bays, and another three were coloured with splashes of white. They danced and fretted, arching their necks in front of the delighted courtiers.

The grooms lined the stallions up against the far wall and then the trumpets sounded once more and through the doors came the six chosen mares. My heart stopped beating. At the front of the herd, champing at the bit and tossing her head high, was none other than my very own Cara.

Oh, Cara! I had thought that I had nothing more to be taken from me. Now I realise in my despair that I was wrong. I left the grand court and ran.

## 22nd September, 1493

As I descended the stairs to the dungeons I could hear the pitiful cries of men wailing or babbling to themselves like madmen. Some of them grabbed at me as I went past, their filthy arms stretching out through the iron bars.

I had promised myself I would be strong, but when I reached my father's cell and saw him crouched there on the cold, stone floor his wrists and ankles clamped with manacles, I couldn't help but weep.

"Felipa!" My father was horrified to see me. "My child! You should not be here!"

"Neither should you!" I choked back my tears. "Father, I am going to get you out of here. If Princess Joanna will not help me then I will seek an audience with the Queen to ask for your freedom…"

"No!" My father's face darkened. "You will not. For even while I am clasped in chains, I am still your father and I forbid it."

"But Father…"

"Do not argue, Felipa!" he said. "You know that to speak out against Tomas de Torquemada is to give yourself a death sentence."

"I can't stand by and let you die!" I sobbed.

"Felipa," my father sighed. "There is no hope for me. They will torture me until I confess. And then, my dear Felipa, they will come after you…"

"But you said yourself that we are under the protection of the Queen!"

My father laughed bitterly. "And look where it has got me!"

I stretched my arms out to comfort him and as our fingertips touched through the iron bars, I saw the look he gave me. There was such love in his eyes it made me feel wretched to think that all this time I had not realised how deeply he had always cared for me.

"You are a Converso, and you too have Jewish blood," my father said. "It is not safe here, Felipa. You must leave the city now."

I was sobbing so hard I couldn't speak.

"Raise your head and let me look upon you," my father said.

I did as he instructed and he smiled.

"My beautiful Felipa. When I close my eyes for the last time, I will picture your face and know that you are safe and I will be happy."

Then his voice turned gruff.

"Now go! Quickly! To be here in the dungeons is already treason. Tomas de Torquemada will send his men after you."

"Yes, Papa." I stood up and made my way towards the stairs. And that was when he said his final words.

"Be careful, Felipa," he whispered. "If they catch you, they will kill you."

The doors to my parents' house had been left wide open since the Inquisition took my father away. I closed it and barred myself inside but even so I scarcely felt safe in my home now. It was late and I managed to heat a humble meal of soup and bread and retired to my room and slept fitfully. I rose again before dawn and entered my parents' bedroom. My father's possessions were just as he had left them. I grabbed his travelling bag and threw in his boots and a waistcoat, an old shirt and trousers. Then I went to my bedroom and took my diary, then finally to my sewing basket where I grabbed my best pair of dressmaking shears that were a gift from my mother. I shoved them into the bag and then I left.

Tomas de Torquemada was sure to hear about my visit to the dungeons soon enough. My father's words rang in my ears as I sprinted across the courtyards of the Alhambra towards the stables.

If they catch you, they will kill you.

I prised open the massive stable doors and hurried down the long, dark corridors. The bag bounced hard against my spine with every stride I took. I had seen guards marching across the pavilion. And I knew that I didn't have much time.

I ran down the cobbled corridor until I reached the very last stall. I fell upon the door, working the bolt with shaking hands, and then stepping inside.

"Cara!" I hissed her name in the gloom. She was a black silhouette in the shadows, moving towards me. Then the light of the window bathed her face and I saw those blue eyes, as clear as the sky.

"My Cara Blanca!" I threw my arms round her and she nickered and shook her mane joyfully. Then I threw the bag on to the straw of the loose-box floor.

"Cara, they are right behind me. We do not have much time!"

I began to undress, easing myself free of my corset, letting my gown fall to the floor. I dropped to my knees, pulled the tangle of garments out from my bag and began my transformation with the roll of mutton cloth, binding myself flat. Over the mutton cloth I put on my father's shirt and waistcoat. I pulled on his trousers, cinched them with a belt and tucked them into the riding boots.

The old clothes I shoved into the bag and then I moved over to the window.

"There is nothing here for me now," I murmured to Cara Blanca. "All I have in the world is you and they will not take you away from me. I will do whatever I must for us to be together. If I cannot change the mind of the Queen then I must change my own fate instead…"

And then I took out the shears…

Footsteps!

This was it. I had to do it now.

Raising the metal blades with my right hand I reached behind my head and grasped my long dark hair, gathering it up tightly and then, in one clean slice, I made the cut. The blade was razor sharp and it did its work masterfully. My waist-length hair had been severed. I now had the blunt bobbed haircut that befitted a young man. In my left hand, I held the shank of my black hair, thick and glossy like a horse's tail. I shoved it roughly into the bag along with the shears.

I hastily tied the bag shut. I could hear the guards working the bolts to the door. This was the moment of reckoning. The door swung open and I was bathed in blinding overwhelming light.

"You!" the guard said. "You, boy! Are you the groom for this horse?"

I felt my heart pounding in my chest. "Yes, sir," I said, trying to make my voice sound low and manly. "Yes, I am."

"Then you will accompany this beast with Admiral Columbus?"

Stay calm, the voice in my head was saying. Speak no more than necessary.

155

"Yes, I will." I slung my bag over my shoulder, and placed the halter and lead rope upon Cara.

"Then saddle up and prepare for the ride to Cadiz," the guard said. "Columbus sets sail upon the morrow on the outgoing tide and your ship to the New World awaits."

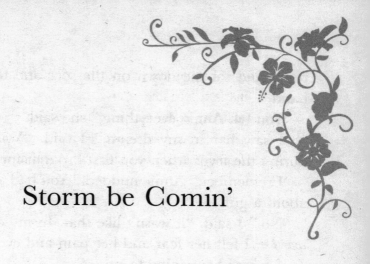

# Storm be Comin'

I must have looked like I'd seen a ghost when I walked into Annie's kitchen. I had Felipa's diary clutched tight in my hands and I was shaking. I felt like it had suddenly got very cold. What was that phrase Mom used to say? *As if someone had walked over your grave.* Well that was how I felt, like someone was stomping over it in fact.

"Lord above, child!" Annie put down the bread she'd been kneading and wiped her hands on her apron. "What be wrong wit you?"

"Annie... I know her!" I said. "I know the girl who wrote this diary."

Annie looked at me, real serious all of a sudden, and then she beckoned me back into the living

157

room and sat me down on the sofa and took my hand.

"You tell Annie everything," she said.

"I saw her in my dream," I said. "You know, during the fever when you first brought me here?"

"I remember," Annie nodded. "You had a dream about a girl…"

"No," I said, "it wasn't like that. In my dream I *was her*. I felt her fear and her pain and everything as if it was happening to me…"

I held up the ancient diary so that Annie could see the battered gold initials on the cover.

"*F* and *M*," I said. "*Felipa Molina*. It's the same girl. I didn't know for sure until I read the diary entry for the twenty-second of September, but it's all in there! Everything that happened in my dream – the stables in Spain, the beautiful mare, the soldiers coming for me – it all really happened to her!"

I clasped the diary tight in my shaky hands, afraid to open it again and even more afraid to put it down. "Annie, how can I be her and me at the same time?" I said. "Felipa lived in fourteen-ninety-three… "

Annie reached out and put her arms round me. "So what now? You think you must be crazy?"

I nodded.

Annie held me close. "Child, ain't notink crazy about you. You be *special*, dat what you is. You got de obeah. De Medicine Hat, she be powerful wit de obeah and you is too, you is connected to her."

A tear ran down my cheek and I sniffled hard, trying not to cry.

"I'm sorry," I said. "I don't know why I'm upset."

"It's OK." Annie gave me a squeeze. "It's scary bein' different and special, it ain't ever easy. But you been different all your life, Bee-a-trizz. There was always sometink callin' out from inside of you. And now de horse, she feel it too and she be callin' back to you."

She reached up and brushed away my tears. Her touch on my skin was so gentle and kind. Just like she'd been with me that day after the mud hole when she stroked my brow and cared for me.

"Bee-a-trizz," she said, "tings are goin' to get real tough in de next few days. You gonna need to be brave, child, and strong too, plenty strong. You got sent to me for a reason, Bee-a-trizz. Annie knew it de moment she laid eyes on you."

I took a deep breath. I was still clutching the diary

tight, but my hands were no longer shaking. Annie was right. I had to be strong now. "What do I have to do?" I said.

Annie stood up. "First-all, we make lunch. Dem grits ain't gonna cook demselves. Den you and me, we got some yard work to do."

"Yard work?" I screwed up my face. It hardly sounded like I was on a sacred mission. It was more like I was doing odd jobs around the house!

Annie walked over to the front porch and stared out at the horizon. "Time to get ready, Bee-a-trizz," she said. "De storm be comin'."

I stared out at the horizon. The sky was clear blue, just like always. "A storm?"

"It's comin', Bee-a-trizz," Annie insisted. "Not far away. Maybe another day or two is all. Dey say it's de big one dis time. When it strikes de coast, ain't notink goin' to survive."

I thought about the Duchess and her herd out on the open unsheltered Bonefish Marshes. Back before the last storm struck, Annie said there were as many as thirty horses. Now there were just eight. If the herd stayed where they were, they would never survive.

"We have to get the horses to safety," I said, "move them away from the beach until it passes."

"Sure 'nuff, child," Annie nodded. "Dey be safe here in de pens. But first we need to do some yard work. Gots to get de fences strong enough to hold dem…"

Making Annie's ramshackle animal pens secure enough to hold the horses was a big job, and the sun was already past its highest point. Mom had only let me take the Zodiac on the condition that I would be back by dinnertime.

"I…" I had to leave, but I couldn't get the words out. Annie needed me. If I didn't stay and help, she would never get this place ready in time.

"…I want to help," I said.

Annie grunted her approval. "Den we get started…"

It had been a long time since Annie last went to a hardware store. Her tools were a very rusty handsaw, an ancient hammer and a single pack of nails. There were no milled planks of timber either, just bits of old driftwood and fallen tree branches.

Annie got me doing the demolition work first – getting rid of the bits of the pens that were rotten and weak; ripping the old, damaged boards off with my hammer – while she cooked us grits.

After we'd eaten lunch, she did the washing-up and then came out to help me with the pens, preparing the new boards to be nailed up.

All the time she was working, Annie kept on talking. She asked lots of questions. I don't know how she got me talking about Kristen Adams, but soon I was telling her everything.

"We were best friends," I said. "Now she never returns my emails."

I expected Annie to be sympathetic, but she wasn't.

"Maybe she ain't got notink to say?"

"Sure she does," I replied. "She has loads of things to write about – she has lots of friends and she goes to parties and stuff."

"So you want her to write to you and brag about her life and all de good stuff you be missing?" Annie said. "Some friend she be den!"

I remembered how Kristen's emails used to make me feel. Every time she mentioned some new friend that she was hanging out with or going to the mall or any of the things we used to do that I couldn't be a part of any more, it gave me pangs. Sometimes so badly that I didn't reply to her for days afterwards. I guess Kristen sensed it too. In the end there was nothing we could say to each other that didn't hurt. Maybe that was the real reason she stopped writing to me.

"Maybe not," I admitted, "but it just… it gets lonely, you know? Being out here."

Annie examined the piece of driftwood in her hand. "You still got your mama."

I sighed. "Mom's OK, I guess; she… well, she just doesn't *get me*, you know? She thinks that I keep asking to go live with Dad just to annoy her."

Annie pouted out her lips to point at the hammer on the ground beside me. "Carry me de hammer, will you?"

I picked it up and passed it over. She hit a nail in to hold the board steady. "Bee-a-trizz," she said, "you remember how de stallion attacked you on de Bonefish Marshes?"

"Uh-huh."

"Den you see de way de Duchess she done come a-flyin' outta nowhere? She throwin' herself between you and de stallion."

"That wasn't what happened," I said. "The Duchess knocked me over because she wanted to fight…"

Annie shook her head. "Annie saw it all, Bee-a-trizz. Dat horse pushed you aside and saved your life. She be protectin' you."

"Protecting me?" I said.

Annie grunted. "Child, sometimes it be hard to tell who's tryin' to hurt you and who's tryin' to save you."

And I knew she wasn't talking about the Duchess any more.

***

All the time we'd been working on the pens the sun had been baking hot. I must have drunk a whole gallon of switcher all by myself, I was so thirsty. I kept thinking about Mom and how I should be heading back to the boat.

Annie had run out of nails and I had to use rope instead to bind railings to the posts. And there was still a big gap in the fenceline that needed patching up before it would be secure.

"We needs to gather up more wood," she said. "Get some big pieces and cut dem up. Den come day-clean once de pens are done we start on de crib. Got to nail all de windows shut."

"You mean tomorrow?" I said. "Annie, I need to go home. My mom will be worried."

164

"Ain't no way we'll get de job done in one day," Annie said. "I need your help, Bee-a-trizz."

"OK," I said reluctantly. "I guess I better phone my mom."

Mom had insisted that I take the spare phone from the *Phaedra*. Reception wasn't good, but it was a clear enough signal to hear a dial tone. I let it ring five, six, seven times and then Mom answered.

"Beatriz! Is that you? What's wrong?"

"Nothing is wrong, Mom. I just got held up. I've been helping Annie out. There's too much to do so I'm going to have to stay here the night. I'll come back in the morning, OK?"

"You're at Annie's?" I could tell Mom was horrified. "Sweetie, that old woman is as mad as a cut snake! I told you not to go there."

"She's not, Mom. And I'm OK, I'll be home first thing tomorrow, I promise."

"Beatriz," Mom said, "listen to me. There's a hurricane warning on the marine forecast. I need you to get back to the boat. Where are you?"

"I'm at Annie's cottage. It's in the jungle, about a half-mile inland past Saw Mill Sink."

"Saw Mill Sink!" Mom said. "Beatriz, that's on the other side of the island!"

"I know," I said. "I'll be home tomorrow, Mom, I promise. The pens are almost finished. We just have to storm-proof the house and then straight after that I'll come home, OK? I gotta go now, I don't want the phone to die."

"No! Beatriz. Listen to me…"

I could tell Mom was going to get shouty so I rang off. I knew I shouldn't, but she isn't always right, is she?

\*\*\*

By evening we had almost finished the pens. They weren't pretty but they were solid. Or at least I hoped they would be. The hurricane that was coming was strong enough to rip trees out of the ground.

"Less wind here," Annie insisted. "Safer here. I been here for forty years. Dat's a whole lot o' hurricanes."

Annie's storm shutters were made from thick chunks of Caribbean pine. We spent the remaining hours of daylight preparing them. Tomorrow morning we would fit and nail them on to the windows of her house.

"You like okra?" Annie asked as we walked

166

back to the house. "I got the pot boiling for dinner."

I had never eaten okra before, but it turned out that I did. I drank a whole lot more switcher and Annie made us a pot of gumbo-limbo tea, which she infused from the bark of a tree right outside the front door. It tasted kind of licoricey.

"Where you put de diary?" Annie asked.

"It's in my backpack," I said.

She picked up the backpack and passed it to me and then settled herself down beside me on the sofa.

"Open it up, Bee-a-trizz," she said. "You're gonna read to me."

While we were working on the pens, I had recounted Felipa's diary so that Annie was up to date on the story so far.

"In the last entry, she had been found by the guards in Cara's stable," I recapped. "Now she's just left the Alhambra on her way to join Christopher Columbus on his new voyage."

Annie lay back on the sofa and shut her eyes. "Wait a moment. Annie's gettin' comfy," she said. "Been a long time since anyone read me a story. Not since I was a little piccaninny."

Annie folded her hands in her lap and gave me a nod. I opened up the diary and began to read out loud…

# F.M.

## 24th September, 1493

Such a sight greeted me at the port of Cadiz! Never in my life have I seen so many ships put to sea at once. Fifteen caravels were anchored out in the bay, and the sea surrounding these great ships was alive with rowing boats, busily ferrying supplies from the wharves.

The biggest ships were the two carracas – triple-masted sailing ships moored alongside the wharf – and the sailors were loading these with sacks of corn and grain. Such repulsive men! Fat-bellied with blackened teeth and whiskery, weather-beaten skin. They scurried about the decks like rats, running up the riggings and hoisting the mainsails. Their shouting and swearing would have made a lady blush.

But I was not a lady any more.

"You, boy!" I turned round to see a broad-shouldered man dressed in tall boots, a billowing white shirt and a wide hat with a feather plume in the brim glaring at me.

"Are you on this crew?"

I tried to deepen my voice as best I could. "Yes, sir," I said. "I am the groom of this horse for the journey."

Cara Blanca was pulling so hard against the lead rope in my hands I was having trouble holding on to her. She had never been so close to the sea before and she kept shying at the sight of the white-tipped ocean waves that slapped hard against the sides of the carracas.

"Sir? Hah! Such fancy speech!" the man laughed at me. "I can tell you're no sailor."

"No, sir," I said.

"Stop calling me sir and address me as boatswain!" the man replied. "And you're not a groom any more either. You'll be ship's boy... not much else you're fit for..."

Cara continued to fret and pull against the rope. My arms were aching and I did not think I could hold her for much longer.

"Well come on then, scrawny boy!" the boatswain growled. "Get this beast onboard with the others!"

A wooden ramp had been laid across from the wharf to the deck of the carraca and I led my horse over to it.

"Step up, girl," I whispered to her. "It's going to be OK. You can do it..."

I managed to coax Cara to take a step forward, and then another, but when she reached the centre of the ramp she looked down and saw the roiling froth of the open sea beneath her and pulled back in horror.

"Cara!" She wrenched the rope clean from my hands. As she flung herself backwards, I thought she would fall into the sea! On the wharf, men carrying baskets of Seville oranges had to leap aside to avoid being trampled by her.

I made a grab and caught her by the halter. "Hold her," the boatswain growled. He had a thick piece of wood in his hands.

"Please, no! Don't hit her!" I begged him.

The boatswain scowled. "Get her onboard then!"

I was shaking all over as I led Cara forward to the edge of the ramp once more. "Come on," I pleaded. "For me, Cara, please!"

She would not step up.

"Enough of this nonsense!" The boatswain lunged closer. "This'll get her on!"

He was about to bring the lump of wood down hard when I saw a hand appear out of nowhere and clasp the boatswain's wrist.

"What the...?" the boatswain exclaimed. "Let me go!"

171

He shook himself free and now I could see a young sailor boy, not much older than me, standing behind him. He was a skinny lad. But when he spoke his voice had such assurance, as if he were used to addressing men as his equal.

"Boatswain," the young sailor boy said, "a beating will not convince this horse to get onboard."

"Is that so?" the boatswain chuckled at his impudence. "Well then, able seaman, let me see you do better!"

The Boatswain stood aside and the sailor boy made his way over to me. He gave Cara a pat and then reached down and unwrapped the scarf that he wore round his waist.

"Tie this round your mare's eyes," he whispered. "Go on, do it quickly or this great fool will beat her half to death!"

I did as the boy said, wrapping the scarf round Cara's head so that she was completely blindfolded.

"Now lead her forward again," the boy instructed. He saw me hesitate and smiled. "It's OK," he insisted. "She will go on this time, I promise."

Sure enough, with the blindfold to protect her from the sight of the gaping void beneath the ramp, Cara was no longer afraid. Her hooves clattered on the wood as she stepped onboard and then down another ramp that led us below deck.

It was here in the bowels of the ship that the grim reality of the voyage that lay ahead of us struck me. The animals were crowded and already the stench was unbearable.

The mares were crammed in so close that they had been attacking each other. A few had open bite wounds on their necks. One poor unfortunate had been bitten on the eye and it was seeping and swollen. The worst injury by far though was a poor mare who had been kicked so hard and at such an angle that her hind leg dangled painfully from the stifle.

"We must unload that horse!" I said to the boatswain. "The leg looks broken."

"I'm loading the boat, not unloading," the boatswain said.

"But she's in pain!" I said.

"Let her suffer! It makes no mind to me!"

"But if it is broken," I reasoned, "then she is no good for work or for breeding."

The boatswain bent down to look at the leg and then gave a dismissive grunt. "Then we'll use her for meat."

I was utterly horrified! He meant to eat this poor horse?

"You are nothing but a—" I was about to let loose when I felt a sharp blow to my guts. The kind, young sailor boy who had given me his scarf had just punched me in the stomach!

I fell to the floor gasping, unable to breathe. I heard the boatswain's laughter as he stomped away.

"Up you get then!" The boy held his hand out to me. I refused to take it. I struggled up without his help.

"You expect me to take your hand? You punched me!"

"You can thank me later," the sailor boy said. "I was saving your life."

"By felling me to the ground?"

"By keeping you quiet in front of that great oaf," the boy replied. "What do you think would've happened if you'd given tongue to your feelings just now? The boatswain would have used his lump of wood to beat you to death."

The boy took back his scarf and tied it round his waist. Then he stuck out his hand to me once more.

"My name is Juan," he said. "And you are?"

"Felipa… I mean, Felipe," I said. I shook his hand reluctantly. He was a sailor, after all.

Juan looked at me with a curious expression. He examined my hand and then said, "You ever sailed before, Felipe?"

"No," I admitted.

"Then what brings you on this journey?" he asked.

"I… want to serve my Queen by travelling to the New World," I said.

Juan laughed. "How worthy you are! I only wanted to get out of Spain."

He smiled at me. "Come on. I can see you are worried about your horse. If we arrange the hay bales between your mare and the others, she will have some space to herself."

"Thank you, kind sir," I said. As soon as the words tumbled from my mouth I regretted them. I had to start talking like a ship's boy or I would be found out before we even left the port! Luckily Juan didn't seem to notice. He turned to leave.

"Excuse me," I said. "Could you show me to my room?"

Juan laughed again. "We have no rooms here! We sleep above deck under the stars."

"Oh." I had been expecting my own private quarters.

"You can take the hammock that is strung above mine if you like," Juan said. "You are a skinny lad and I would prefer to have you fall upon me in the middle of the night if there is a storm. Most of the crew are so fat they would crush me alive..."

As we stood on deck I could feel the boat swaying and rocking. I felt like throwing up.

"Does it always move like this?"

"Felipe," Juan said, "we have not even left port yet!"

He looked hard at me. "This journey will be too tough for someone like you. Take my advice – get off this ship now. Before it is too late."

"I cannot," I replied. "I have nowhere else to go."

Juan sighed. "Come on then, Felipe," he said. "There are fifty barrels of wine to be loaded onboard and the boatswain will not be pleased if he finds us slacking."

# F.M.

## 27th September, 1493

There are seventeen ships bound for the New World. And yet, incredibly, I managed to board the one captained by Admiral Columbus himself.

The admiral is hardly ever seen on deck – he keeps himself in his cabin with his maps and charts. Today, however, my luck ran out.

"Cabin boy," the boatswain said, "take the admiral his meal."

"Me?"

"Yes, boy! You!"

And so I found myself entering the captain's cabin where

176

Admiral Columbus was at the table, examining his navigation instruments.

"Admiral, I have brought your lunch."

I tried to put the plate down swiftly and leave before he noticed me.

"Wait, boy!" I was at the door when he called me back to him.

"Give this to the boatswain," he said, handing me a rolled-up chart.

I made to leave but the admiral's hand did not release the parchment. I froze. He was staring at me with a puzzled expression on his face.

"Do I know you, boy? Have you crewed for me before?"

"No, Admiral," I replied. I could feel a trickle of sweat running down the back of my neck. Would he recognise me as the giggling companion of Princess Joanna? I held my breath. He looked as if he was about to say something. Then he changed his mind and let go of the chart.

"Be off then."

So I am safe — for now, at least. But in future I shall stay out of the admiral's way. My haircut and garments have fooled him once, but he is a clever man and my disguise will not trick him forever.

## 30th September, 1493

We eat a hot meal once a day at 11am. The cook stirs a pot over hot coals and then dishes it up on our plates. The sailors bolt down their share like pigs at a trough. At first I was too repulsed to eat. Then I realised that my behaviour was arousing suspicion and so I did exactly the same as the others, scoffing my food straight from the plate without cutlery.

The boatswain is the worst of them. He belches and farts constantly and his breath is like the sewer. He hates me too. At first he set me the worst tasks on the ship: cleaning out the bilge in the belly of the boat, which is the most disgusting job you could imagine, bucketing out the slop and toilet waste. This lasted a few days until he found a new way of tormenting me.

"A scrawny boy like you is not good for much," the boatswain told me, "except for climbing the rigging."

Now I am sent up the ropes each day like a trained monkey. Even in the very worst weather imaginable, rain lashing my skin and gusts of wind threatening to blow me off the mast and into the sea, I must climb my way up the rungs until I have reached the lookout at the top of the mast. Sometimes I stay there for hours on end, the sun beating down mercilessly upon me as I watch the horizon for signs of land. The rocking of the ship is even worse atop the mast and when the winds get high it is terrifying.

On hot days the crew all strip to their waist in the sun. I am the only one to keep my shirt on.

"Come on, Felipe," Juan teases me with a wry grin. "Why not feel the sea breeze on your skin?"

Sometimes I notice Juan looking at me and when our eyes meet he does not look away — instead he smiles at me!

Most of the sailors are uncouth and none can read. Only Juan takes books to bed with him every night. He reads out loud. I can hear him muttering the words in the bunk beneath me.

"Why do you read like that?" I ask him.

"We have a new world ahead of us, Felipe," Juan says. "I am teaching myself to read. I plan to become a learned man."

"I am already well educated," I sniff.

"Then you can become anything you want to be," Juan smiles at me, "or anyone."

What I want most is to be a girl again. At night I lie on my bunk with my bag tucked under my head as a makeshift pillow. My chest feels like it will burst out from beneath the gauze bandages that still bind me. How long can this voyage last?

# F.M.

## 24th October, 1493

*Oh, how sick I feel!*

I can barely hold my quill to write these words. For six days now the storms have wracked the ship. By day I am forced to carry out my duties, unable to stomach any food or drink. By sunset I am exhausted, and yet I find it impossible to sleep. With each surge and swell of the sea I retch over the side of my bunk.

My beloved Cara fares just as badly as I do. I visit her every day in the bowels of the ship. The stench is so bad I gag and cannot breathe. I try to tempt her to eat her hay and to drink the fresh water I have brought her. She takes tiny sips, and barely touches her feed and the look on her face makes my heart break.

She is a noble horse, from the finest bloodlines, and she was never intended for such a journey. And yet here we both are, out at sea, with no sign of land, and with the food and drink on our ship now running in short supply. Tonight at dinner the biscuits were alive and crawling with weevils and the salted meat had begun to rot a little. Still, I ate my share. I must keep up my strength. Who knows how long it might be before we reach the New World?

## 30th October, 1493

Last night Juan stopped reading his book and stuck his head over my hammock.

"What is that you are always writing?" he asked.

"I keep a diary," I told him.

"Can I read it?" he asked.

"Certainly not!" I replied. "It is private."

Juan was disappointed. "What's it about then?" he said.

"Me – my life," I said.

"Tell me about your life, Felipe," Juan said.

And so I did, in a way. I told him about my mother's death and my father's imprisonment at the hands of Tomas de Torquemada. I missed out some parts, of course – I didn't tell of Princess Joanna's refusal to help me. Now that I am away from Spain and no longer fear the charge of treason,

I can write what I truly feel about Joanna. It hurts my heart greatly when I think of her. I had considered her my dearest friend, a sister, but when I needed her most she abandoned me. I want to hate her — but all I feel is pity. I know Joanna's heart too well. She will regret what she has done to me — her betrayal will be a torment that eats away at her soul.

"What about your story?" I said to Juan.

"There is nothing to tell," he insisted. "I do not dwell on my past. It is the future that excites me. When we reach the New World I will be given my own land to care for and I shall raise animals and plant crops and have horses, lots of horses."

"That sounds nice," I said.

Juan smiled. "I am glad you think so."

He gazed at me, his eyes fixed on mine.

"Why are you looking at me strangely?" I asked him.

"No reason," Juan said. "Good night, Felipe."

"Good night, Juan."

## 31st October, 1493

When I woke this morning the sky was tinged with crimson.

"It is a bad sign," Juan said. "Red night, shepherd's delight, red morning — sailor's warning."

Sure enough, soon there was thunder in the air. The red skies clouded black and the sea began to churn.

The waves rose up to such a height they threatened to swamp the ship, and the rain fell so hard that it drenched my clothes and stung my cheeks.

Yet still the boatswain ordered me to climb the mast to the lookout.

"Get up there, boy!" he shouted at me above the wind. "Be my eyes and tell me what you see!"

"In this weather?" I was horrified. "The rain is too dense. All I shall see is the storm engulfing us!"

"Do you defy me, boy?" the boatswain roared. "Get up there now!"

And so I grasped the wet ropes in my hands and I climbed up, one rung after the other, hanging on for dear life as the ship lurched and pitched with every wave that struck the bow.

Halfway up the mast, I looked down and realised the madness of the task I had been set. I could barely see the deck! How on earth would I possibly see to the horizon?

"Sir!" I shouted through the storm. "I can't see a thing! I—"

At that moment a rogue wave struck the carraca with such force that I was thrown into mid-air. As I fell, I managed to grasp on to a sail rope, sliding my way down. There was a searing pain as the rope burnt my hands, but I clung on. Freefalling would mean certain death and the rope slowed me just enough to save my life. All the same, I hit the deck hard and I must have struck my head because everything went black.

When I woke again, there was no more storm. I was inside the doctor's cabin on a bunk and I was in dry clothes. I should have been grateful that I was alive, and that I had been taken care of. Instead, I was terrified. Someone had undressed me and changed me into dry things. And in doing so they must have seen the bindings on my chest!

I clutched at my shirt. "Oh, no! Oh, no!"

"It's all right."

It was Juan.

"Nobody saw anything," he told me. "I was the one who carried you here and changed your clothes. So you see, you are safe. No one knows your secret except me."

I looked at him astonished, and a little afraid. "What will you do? Now that you know what I really am?"

Juan shook his head. "Oh, Felipa!" he laughed. "I have known that you were a girl from the first day we met!"

He stood up beside my bunk and reached out to take my hand in his own.

"It was your hands that gave you away – so slender and beautiful. Who else but a noblewoman would have such delicate, milk-white fingers?"

He turned my hand over and opened my palm, all red and raw from the rope burns. "Here," he said, "I have some salve for your burns…"

I gasped as the ointment touched the wounds. "You knew all this time? Why did you not confront me?"

Juan smiled. "And miss the chance to watch you try to behave like a ship's boy? Why should I tell you and ruin my fun?"

# Abandoned

I was supposed to leave at dawn, but every time I talked about going home Annie found something new to add to the list of chores.

By lunchtime we'd completely rebuilt the pens and even hammered up a solid wall of timber on one side to block the incoming wind. Then we put up the storm shutters and boarded up the cottage windows.

Finally, I couldn't see anything else that needed doing. Then Annie said she wanted me to go with her to the Bonefish Marshes.

"Annie, I can't!" I told her. "I need to get back to the *Phaedra*. Mom is going to be beside herself…"

Annie grunted. "Can't get dem horses back on ma own, Bee-a-trizz. I need your help, child. De horses need your help. If we go now we can be back by nightfall."

I groaned. "Mom is going to kill me…"

"Yes, she is!"

I turned round and there – standing in the middle of Annie's yard next to the bottle tree – was Mom.

She looked exhausted. She had on her tramping boots and a backpack. She must have come overland through the jungle – there was no other way for her to get here since I had taken the Zodiac.

"Mom?"

"Beatriz," Mom took off her backpack and let it drop to the ground, "do you realise what you have put me through? I have been out of my mind with worry! I must have criss-crossed this island three times trying to track you down! Luckily I spotted the Zodiac on the mudflats and from there I saw the tyre tracks through the jungle leading me here… I thought I would never find you!"

Annie turned to me. "Bee-a-trizz? I thought you phoned your mama to say you were safe?"

"Safe?" My mom's joy was very quickly being replaced by outrage. "You're not safe here, Beatriz! There is a storm coming. Not just a little one – a hurricane. They're saying that it will sweep across the whole of the Bahamas in about twenty-four hours..."

"I know!" I said. "But I had to help Annie..."

"Annie can't stay here either!" Mom said. "She has to come with us. When that storm strikes the winds will reach one hundred and fifty miles per hour. It doesn't matter how many shutters you put on this shack – it isn't going to be able to stand up to that sort of force!"

Annie looked insulted. "Ma crib ain't no shack. It survive many storms and come out de other side to tell de tale!"

"Look, Annie," Mom backtracked, "all I'm saying is it would be safer if you came with us. We can make it back to the *Phaedra* tonight and then in the morning as soon as it's light we'll go back up the coast to Marsh Harbour. We can moor at the marina and then bring you back home after the storm has passed."

"No!" I said, suddenly realising that there was no way I could leave the Duchess to face this storm without me. "Don't you get it, Mom? Annie's not leaving, and... and I'm not leaving. The horses are still out there. We've got to bring them in off the Bonefish Marshes."

That was when Mom lost it.

"Beatriz!" she said. "Enough of this nonsense! There are no horses here and even if there were, they can look after themselves! They're wild animals, for goodness' sake!"

"They can't!" I said, shaking my head. "Mom, last time there was a hurricane half the herd got killed. And this storm is much, much worse…"

"And that's why *we* must leave!" Mom said. "It's a matter of hours away and it's going to destroy everything in its path. We need to pack up and head for Marsh Harbour."

"I'm not going," I said quietly. "The horses need me."

Mom turned to Annie. "This is your fault," she said. "Filling her head with nonsense! Now, are you coming?"

Annie shook her head. "You can't run from de storm."

"Oh, really?" Mom grabbed her backpack. "Watch me!"

She pulled her pack on and then she stomped over and grabbed me by the arm.

"Ow!" I tried to pull free but she had hold of me really tight. "Mom! You're hurting me!"

"Beatriz," Mom said. "Listen to me. You are coming with me and we are leaving right now. We are going back to get the Zodiac and then we are getting back to the *Phaedra*."

Mom looked at Annie. "I'm asking you for the last time," she said. "I don't want to leave you here, but I can't make you go. It's your choice."

Annie stared back at my mom. "Annie ain't leavin'," she said. "I gots to carry dem horses back. I sure could use help. You can stay here wit' me in ma crib. You be safe here."

"Thank you," Mom said, "but we have to go."

With her hand still gripping my arm, Mom marched me off.

I'd never seen her so angry. She gave me a lecture that didn't stop the whole way back through the jungle. I didn't say a word – and I kept up my silent treatment all the way back to the Zodiac.

"I know what you're doing, Beatriz," Mom said as she pushed the Zodiac into the water and lowered the outboard. "Well, that's fine. But if you think I am leaving you on an island in the middle of a tropical hurricane then you are even crazier than that old woman!"

She was trying to provoke me, but I wasn't going to bite. It wasn't until we were back on the *Phaedra* that I snapped.

"I tell you what, Bee," Mom said cheerfully, trying to act like we were friends again. "Once we get to the marina, how about we stay the night at Wally's? We can rent a room there and call room service for dinner – conch burgers, key lime pie – the works. Would you like that?"

"Ohmygod!" I was horrified. "You think I want room service when my horse is going to be stuck out there in that storm? Do you even realise what you've done, Mom? Those horses are going to die. Annie can't bring the herd in by herself."

"Saving human life is more important," Mom said. "Annie is an adult and she made her choice – she just made the wrong one."

"You think everybody has to do exactly as you say. Like you're the boss of everyone," I said. "Well, you're not. As soon as this is over, you know what I'm gonna do? I'm gonna get on a plane and go back to Florida, and I don't care what you say – I am going to live with Dad!"

"No, you're not!" Mom said.

"Yes, I am!"

"No, you're not!" she shouted. "Because he doesn't want you!"

I saw Mom's face sort of crumple with shock at

her own words. As for me, I couldn't speak. I felt like I couldn't even breathe.

"I'm… I'm sorry, Beatriz," Mom stammered. "I didn't mean to… I should never have said… I'm so sorry…"

"Is it true?"

Mom didn't answer.

"Is it true?!" I was shaking so hard.

"He's got problems, Bee. He can't cope with anything more on his plate."

"So I'm a problem? That's how he sees me?"

All this time with my big talk about going back to Florida and Mom knew all along that Dad didn't want me.

Mom had started crying now. And even more than the shouting that really upset me because my Mom never, ever cries. "I shouldn't have told you," she said. "I lost my temper. I'm sorry…"

I couldn't take any more so I stormed downstairs and threw myself down face first on my bunk.

"Beatriz?" Mom was standing in the doorway, sniffing quietly. I said nothing. I didn't even raise my head.

"We can discuss this later, OK, honey?" Mom said gently. "I have to get the boat ready to go."

Mom stood there for a moment and then she turned and went back up the stairs.

She's still upstairs now. I can hear her up there crashing around, battening down the *Phaedra*, preparing to leave. And I'm lying here on my bunk, writing in my diary.

When I was in Mrs Moskowitz's class, she told us that a diary is a *version* of events. It's never the whole story.

I used to imagine that I had this perfect life just waiting for me in Florida and that Mom was the one to blame for keeping me stuck here. That was my version.

And now I can't pretend it's true any more.

# F.M.

## 21st November, 1493

The boatswain sent me up the mast this afternoon and made me stay up there for hours in the hot sun.

I was desperately thirsty and I was about to beg to be let down when I saw something black on the horizon. It was no more than a speck at first, and I did not dare to mention it for fear of being mocked. So I kept my eye on the speck and very soon it had become a bulge. I knew that my eyes were not deceiving me.

"Land ahoy!"

As soon as the two words left my lips men began shouting. They crowded the deck to the port side and looked out over the sea, trying to catch a glimpse of land. Others began to climb the ropes alongside me. "Out of the way!" the boatswain growled at them as he climbed up with his eyeglass and peered out at the horizon.

"It's true!" he confirmed. "Land ahoy! Less than a day's sail from here!"

There was merriment and dancing on the ship that night. Suddenly the men were full of stories, talking about what they would do when we arrived in the New World. I did not join in their carousing. I ate my ration of weevil-ridden biscuit and rank salted beef and then I went below deck to visit Cara.

Rats scuttled in front of my feet as I made my way through the muck, gagging at the stench. The vermin had grown in numbers during the voyage and they had no fear.

Once I found a fat brown rat gorging himself in Cara's feed bucket while she was trying to eat!

Poor Cara. She has grown so thin on the long voyage. Her muscles have wasted from standing still for so long. Her coat, once so glossy and fine, has fallen out in great patches and her blue eyes are so sad.

"Be strong, my dear Cara!" I whispered excitedly to her as I reached her side, "for I have seen land. In one more day we will be there and all of this will be over."

I stayed with Cara for a long time, brushing her and telling her about the new life that lay ahead of us when we arrived in Hispaniola. When I said good night to her at last tears pricked my eyes as I hugged her tight. "We did it," I murmured to Cara. "We survived the journey, and now, at last, we will be free…"

# F.M.

## 30th November, 1493

Oh, what a naive fool I have been! To think that I truly believed that when we reached the New World, Cara Blanca and I would be safe and happy!

Nothing could be further from the truth.

We arrived here to find that the forty men Columbus had left behind were all dead. Some had been killed fighting with the native people. Others had died from diseases. Behind them they left a legacy of fear and hatred with the local tribesmen.

The colony that Columbus christened Isabella is now in a state of chaos. Sailors are not farmers and they haven't a clue how to settle this land. All they do is fight.

I have taken to hiding myself away from the village settlement. I took my bag and found a quiet sheltered place near a waterfall in the jungle. Here I've built a makeshift shelter out of old ship's canvas bound on to tree branches for me and Cara to share.

I keep Cara with me always. Her strength improves daily. The other horses on our voyage have not been so fortunate. Taken by the sailors, they've been forced straight into hard labour, chained and harnessed to pull logs out of the forest for house building. All this despite the fact that their bones are sticking out through their coats from hunger!

## 13th December, 1493

Even in our hideaway I worry for our safety. The men are hungry and they prowl the island, thieving from each other to survive. The ship's supplies have now completely run out and the settlement has become an evil and dangerous place. Admiral Columbus appears to have lost any control he once had. The fighting grows worse and I now carry a knife with me in my belt and sleep with it at the ready…

## Midnight

I was woken from my sleep to the sound of voices; footsteps creeping close by. It was a pitch-black night and my last candle, my only source of light, had been snuffed out. I reached for my knife, but what good could it do me when I could not even see my hand in front of my face?

"Who's there?" I tried to make my voice deep and fearsome, but the sound that came from my throat was girlish and scared. Then I heard Cara stomp and let out a terrified whinny. They had hold of her! In the cover of darkness they were taking my horse!

"Stop!" I called out for all the good it would do. I could hear the men — there were at least two of them. They had untied her. They were taking my Cara!

I could feel my heart slamming against my ribs as I held out the knife and walked into the darkness.

There! Two silhouettes against the black night sky. "I can see you!" I shouted. "Let go of my horse!"

One of the men laughed. They had her by the rope and she was kicking out wildly. There was nothing I could do.

And then, right in front of them, appeared a dark figure holding a sword aloft.

"Get away from her now!"

I heard the clash and scrape of metal, and a cry of pain. By the time I had reached Cara, the two men were gone and Juan was standing there, holding on to Cara's lead rope and soothing her. I threw my arms round him and hugged him for I had truly thought that Cara was lost.

"It's all right." Juan held me tight. "They will not return. Not tonight at least."

Juan stayed with Cara that night and kept watch. All the same, I did not sleep. I do not think I will ever be able to sleep again. I sat awake and lit the last remnants of my candle to make this entry in my diary. I am watching it, my eyes fixed on the flame as it burns low. It will be gone by dawn. I will face the next night in darkness. I cannot expect Juan to guard me again. And what if the men come back? What then?

## 14th December, 1493

What a horror greeted me this morning! I had gone to fetch some water from the village when I saw the carcass of a beast roasting over an open fire. As I got closer I realised it was not a cow or a pig, but a horse! So that's what the midnight raid had been for! The men had been trying to steal Cara to eat her!

I felt so disgusted, I fell to my knees and threw up. I forgot about the water and ran back to Juan.

"This isn't a new world," I told him. "It is a hell where men kill each other and their animals too. As long as we stay here we shall never be safe. We are leaving."

"And how do you plan to do that?" Juan asked.

"Steal a ship," I said, suddenly struck by the idea. "Take it under cover of darkness... tomorrow night."

Juan stared at me for what felt like hours and then finally said, "Felipa, you are right. This is no place to live. The two of us shall leave together."

I looked at him, quite alarmed. "Not the two of us," I said. "All of us. You, me and Cara, and the other horses too!"

"The other horses?" Juan was shocked. "Felipa, how many do you plan to take with us?"

"All of them," I said.

## 25ᵗʰ April, 2014 - onboard the *Phaedra*

I shouldn't even be writing this. I don't have much time. But if anything should happen to me, then this diary will be the only record of what went on. And Mom, if you are reading this, I want you to know that it wasn't your fault. I'm not doing this because I'm angry at you. I know you were only trying to protect me - I know that's why you never told me the truth about Dad.

I have to go back to Annie's. There's no way she can get the horses to the shelter on her own. They will die if I go with you to Marsh Harbour. So you see, I have no choice.

This must be how Felipa felt when she made the decision to leave Hispaniola. I bet she felt braver than me, though. Mostly right now I am terrified.

I just lowered the Zodiac down into the water. The waves are already getting pretty big and the wind is really gusty. I guess that storm really is coming. The water is choppy and it's pitch black and for just a moment I think about forgetting my plan. A burger and fries at Wally's is sounding pretty good right now...

Mom. If you are reading this, I love you, OK? I'm going to put both diaries in my backpack now and get in the Zodiac and go before I change my mind.

Wish me luck.

Love always, your daughter, Beatriz.

# F.M.

## 5th December, 1493

"It is madness," Juan said when I told him my plan. "Even under the cover of darkness…"

"What choice do we have?" I said. "Leave the horses here to be worked to death or eaten? We must take them all."

Juan sighed. "Then may God protect us! At midnight I shall climb aboard the caravel moored at the jetty and prepare it to set sail. While I'm doing this you gather the mares. Then we will load them together. The stallions will be harder — two at a time is the most you can handle or they will fight. We will load them onboard last and then leave."

\*\*\*

That evening, I sat and plaited bands of flax into a long rope and from this I formed a cobra – a series of headcollars to string on to the mares, tying them together.

By the time the headcollars were finished it was midnight. There was just a fingernail sliver of moon as I set off for the village. I could make out shadows in the darkness but not much else as I crept around the yards. Juan would already be at the jetty preparing the caravel to set sail. Cara waited patiently as I gathered the four other mares. I harnessed Cara at the front and mounted up on her to lead the others.

She fretted and danced beneath me as we set off through the village.

"Shhh, my girl," I soothed her. The soft earth dampened the sound of the mares' hooves. All the same, it was terrifying to lead my procession past the village huts. It would take only one sailor to wake and it would be over.

We came out of the village and down on to the sandy beach. I let the mares trot now, the soft sand muffling their hoofbeats.

It wasn't until we reached the wooden jetty that the clattering of the five mares' hooves on timber echoed dangerously in the night air.

"The village is too far away for them to hear," Juan tried to reassure me as I leapt down from Cara's back and led the mares towards the caravel.

We used Juan's blindfold trick on all five mares and they loaded onboard the small boat easily. We hitched them to the rails, then we went back together on foot to get the stallions.

Death at the hands of the sailors had already claimed two stallions. There were four left and Juan and I had agreed that if we split up then we could each manage two at a time.

At the edge of the village, he gave me a smile and whispered, "See you at the ship." And then he disappeared off into the darkness. Looking back, I wish with all my heart I had said something to him. But how could I have known what was to happen next?

My two stallions – a bay and a pinto – were the property of Columbus, kept in the pens near his dwelling. They gave me no trouble as I put headcollars on both and led them back through the village, down to the beach, across the jetty and all the way to the caravel.

I loaded the stallions onboard, tying them to the forecastle of the caravel, well away from the mares. And then I waited.

Juan's stallions had been on the other side of the village, a little further away than mine, but all the same he was taking too long. Where was he?

The arrival of the stallions on the caravel had made the mares restless. They were stamping and fretting about. Then one of the stallions let out a shrill clarion call.

"Shush!" I told the horses. "Do you want to give us away

with your nonsense?" I went out on to the jetty and paced back and forth, my stomach in a tight knot. Where was Juan? He'd never have taken this long unless…

And then I saw a terrifying sight. On to the beach there emerged a gang of sailors holding lit torches. They were moving swiftly towards the jetty.

Juan!

Oh, where was he?

I could hear the shouts and cries of the sailors. Soon they would be on the jetty. I couldn't wait any longer. I had to go now or I would be taken captive by the mob and my fate would be swift and certain death.

I ran to the side of the caravel and began to untie the mooring ropes. They were heavy and thick, wrapped tight round the wooden posts of the jetty, and my hands worked feverishly to loosen them. I untied the ship at three points and then I heaved as hard as I could on the wooden ramp and let it fall into the water below. We were free of the jetty, but I didn't have much time. The men were closing in.

A caravel is a smaller vessel than the vast carraca on which we had travelled to get here and Juan had already prepared it for departure, hoisting the sails and packing the chests with provisions. All I needed was a gust of wind to catch the mainsail and…

There it was! The sail puffed out and stiffened.

Yes! The caravel was moving!

I grabbed the wheel to steer. We were away from the jetty, but the sailors were not about to give up yet. They were piling into rowing boats and I could hear their cries as they exhorted each other to take the strain!

Pulling in unison, they rowed hard out. They were moving faster than the caravel, swifter than the wind could carry me. I couldn't do a thing. They would catch us before we could leave the bay!

The rowers were preparing to come alongside and board the caravel when suddenly we rounded the point of the bay. The northerly breeze here was strong and powerful. It filled the sails with a sudden gust and as it did so I felt the caravel surge forward, cresting the waves as we sped out of their reach to the open sea!

"We're free, Cara!" I screamed into the wind. "We did it! We're free!"

It wasn't until we had left the men and their rowing boats far behind that I realised what my newfound freedom meant. I was alone on the inky black ocean. On a ship that I didn't know how to sail and without Juan at my side to help me. And that was when I stopped rejoicing and slumped to my knees and cried.

# Night Voyage

The sea was pitch black as I rounded the coastline. I'd tied a torch to the front of the inflatable, thinking it would work like car headlights, but it only lit up a few metres of water, not enough to navigate by.

I could just make out the silhouette of the shoreline and tried to keep close to the dark outline of the land as I came round the rocks at the end of Shipwreck Bay. If I got too far out I would lose my bearings completely. But staying close to the land had its own dangers. At Sandy Point I came right in close to the beach, cutting between two outcrops of reef, and that was when I felt the Zodiac lurch.

The jolt flung me up in the air and almost clear

of the inflatable. I scrambled around, clinging to the wet rubber floor of the boat, trying not to capsize it. I knew that if I stood up, I would tip the whole thing over, so I crawled my way back in the dark until I could grasp the handle on the outboard motor and steady the Zodiac.

I sat up and got my bearings – I was still heading towards the beach. I tried to stay calm but my heart was pounding in my ears. Whatever had caused that bump must have ripped a small hole in the side of the inflatable because the Zodiac was starting to sit real low. By the time I had motored my way round the rocks to Saw Mill Sink the inflatable had taken on so much water that the waves were now coming in over the sides and I was finding it harder and harder to steer.

I made for the shore. The mudflats were just up ahead of me. I could skim the boat over the shallows and try to go inland. It was risky but it was better to crash on the sandbars than to be out at sea in an inflatable that was rapidly sinking.

I tried to steer into the deeper channels but pretty soon I had struck a sandbar and beached myself. I climbed out and dragged the Zodiac back into the water, but when I struck a second sandbar just a few moments later I couldn't get the outboard to start again. I stood there, with the rain coming down hard and tried to kick-start the engine. After about eight tries, I gave up and began to wade.

I was still quite far out on the edge of the flats and I figured the best plan was to find a point on the horizon, like a big tree in the distance, and just head straight for it. If I tried to skirt around the tidal pools I could wind up walking in circles. With the wind steadily gathering at my back, I set out.

The thing is, in the dark, even with a torch, it was impossible to gauge how deep the tidal pools were. Sometimes they only came up to my knees, but other times I found myself in all the way up to my armpits, holding my backpack and torch above my head.

Every now and then, I would catch sight of something in the pools that I wished I hadn't. Spidery crabs and thick, muscular eels, scuttling and slithering to get out of my way. There were silvery bonefish too, shimmering in the water, brushing up against my legs in the deepest trenches, and flatfish darting out from beneath my feet.

Finally the pools became shallower and the mud began to turn sandy. There was more marsh grass swishing about and pretty soon I was walking through creaking mangroves and pigeon berry.

The jungle at night was another world full of screeches and screams as the trees moaned in the wind. I pushed my way through in the dark, using the beam of the torch to light my footing. At one point I heard a hissing noise and when I raised my torch there were green eyes glowing back at me. Whatever it was, it gave another hiss and then scuttled up into the branches of the canopy above me.

When I stumbled on to the tyre tracks I almost wept with relief. It wasn't far now.

The bottle tree was going crazy in the wind when I reached the cottage. "Annie?" I called out. "Annie! It's me!"

I hammered on the door but no one answered. I checked around the side of the house. She had locked the chickens into their coop and the white cat was nowhere to be seen. And the horse pens were empty. I called out Annie's name a few more times but heard nothing back.

The doors to the cottage were unlocked and I knew Annie wouldn't mind if I went inside. I stood in the living room shivering. I could hear the wind rattling at the shutterboards of the old shack – the storm was close. Digging around in my backpack, I took out the two diaries. Mine and Felipa's. I put them side by side on Annie's kitchen table.

Before I left the *Phaedra*, I finished reading Felipa's diary. So now I know the truth about Felipa, and about Cara and what happened that night when they left Hispaniola. And I know that the Duchess is special just like Annie said. That no matter what happens, I have to save her.

I have to go now. In the past few minutes the storm has got much worse. I don't know where Annie is but I do know that the Duchess is still out there. I've borrowed some of Annie's dry clothes. I found a raincoat too. It's pretty smelly, but I figure it'll keep the rain off me. I'm leaving Annie a note to say I've gone to the Bonefish Marshes, just in case she comes back before me. I'm leaving it on the kitchen table along with the diaries – until I return.

# F.M.

## 7th December, 1493

If I am to find land then I must depend on myself. In the captain's cabin there are maps and charts. I was never taught to navigate, but I do know how to read. I've looked through the captain's log and found his notes on the voyage that we had made to Hispaniola and from these I've charted a course. I can't go back the way we came — I'd never make it as far as Spain. Besides, I have only the few provisions onboard that Juan managed to prepare.

So I've set my course due north, away from Hispaniola, heading where the warm ocean currents flow, in the hope that there are undiscovered islands where I might make landfall.

At least the horses seem content. Most of the mares stand side by side and groom each other affectionately, nibbling softly with their teeth. Cara Blanca, however, stands alone, and stares out over the ocean. The last time we were at sea she spent all her time below deck, so the world of water is entirely new to her. I watch her as I steer the ship, admiring her profile as she takes in the scents of the salt air and the cries of the gulls above. She is my boatswain and I am the captain.

## 9th December, 1493

I have only enough water to last the horses perhaps one more day. As for myself, I am now eating Juan's share of our rations.

I miss Juan terribly. Is he still alive? If he were caught taking horses that night then he might have been put to death for theft by those vicious sailors. I dearly hope that instead he escaped and is alive somewhere living in the jungle.

I know he is lost to me and yet each night when I go to sleep it is his face that I see when I close my eyes. This vision comforts me.

I have just checked the water barrel. It is completely empty.

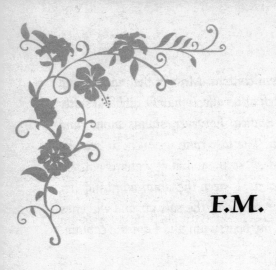

# F.M.

## 10th December, 1493

*Rain!*

This morning when I felt the first drops falling I was so delighted that I ran about the ship laughing and whooping and dancing with my arms open wide. Then, once I was soaking wet, I realised that I was wasting precious time and I hurriedly ran about putting out every bucket and bowl and vessel that might catch water for the horses to drink. I also lowered the mainsail and used that as a giant water-catcher. In a very short time I had enough water for all of the horses and to fill three barrels in reserve.

I almost cried with joy as I watched Cara drink her fill

and then snort playfully, flicking her muzzle in the bucket. We are saved.

## 11th December, 1493

It has rained throughout the night, and as the day progressed the rain became harder still. I watched the winds grow in strength and whip the sails about with such fury, I thought they might rip clean off the masts.

My horses had no shelter. When the skies above us roared with thunder and the sea made the ship rise and pitch, I could see they were terrified, but there was nothing I could do. I had to try to keep the caravel on course.

The winds were freezing cold and as wave after wave came over the bow of the ship I was soaked to the skin.

When I sighted the island in the distance, I screamed, "Land ahoy!" even though there was no one to hear my voice except my horses. The storm was raging all around us by then and it was hard to see what lay ahead.

The winds pushed us towards the shore, but the waves seemed to fight against us and thrust us away. I kept the wind at my back and steered again towards a bay. We were close enough now that I could see a beach, the sandy shore arcing like a horseshoe ahead of us.

We were going to make it!

"Cara!" I called out to my faithful boatswain. "We have done it! We are—"

And that was when I felt the tremor, like an earthquake beneath me. I was thrown across the deck so hard that I thought I would fall off the side of the ship. The caravel lurched to the right, and then banked to the left so steeply that the sails dipped to the water. We had struck rocks beneath the surface at full speed!

I left the ship's wheel and made my way below deck. The hull had split clean open like a coconut and we were taking on water fast!

I got back on deck as swiftly as I could. The caravel was listing to the left and it was hard to stand up. I kept falling over and slipping as I fought my way to the starboard side. The poor horses were still tethered to the railings by their ropes and they were scrambling about as the ship lurched in the swell. Unless I cut them loose, they would go down with this ship.

I was halfway across the deck when the caravel gave another sickening lurch. I screamed and threw myself flat against the deck, then began to crawl the rest of the way on my belly, clinging to the boards with my fingers, holding on for dear life.

I ended up nearest to one of the stallions and I had to be

careful not to be kicked as I edged my way up beside him. I had just pulled my knife out from my belt and was about to saw through his ropes when the ship gave another lurch. I screamed again as I was thrown hard against the railings. The stallion's ropes saved me, otherwise I would have been thrown overboard. The ship righted itself briefly, creaking horribly as it did so, and I could stand again. We were low in the water, sinking further and further.

I cut through the stallion's ropes and as soon as he was free he barged right past me, breaking through the railing with his front legs and plummeting down into the churning seas below. I watched him sink beneath the waves and then, in a great burst he broke the surface once more! He looked like a sea serpent, with only his head and neck above the mighty waves. He began swimming, his legs making huge thrusts, his ears pricked forward at the sight of the shoreline ahead of him.

"That's it!" I shouted after him. "Swim! Swim!"

I cut the next stallion loose and then started on the mares, who were grouped further along the railing. By now the waves were washing over the bow.

Luckily, because the mares were tied in a cobra, all I had to do was release the main rope with swift cuts and they were free.

All except Cara. She was at the far end of the row by

herself. The last rope that I needed to cut. By the time I reached her she was stamping and frothing, desperate to follow the others. My knife was blunted and I had to saw at the rope that held her headcollar. I had just cut through the last strands when I heard the creak of wood splitting and turned just in time to see the mast fall.

It came down like a tree felled in the forest – so fast and so violent, it was impossible to get out of the way. The thick wooden pole missed me, but I was struck by the sail and the next thing I knew I was being dragged over the side of the caravel. Caught in the ropes and canvas, trapped like a fish in a net, I was swept off the deck and into the sea below.

The blow of the sail had winded me. I inhaled seawater and choked on it, coughing hard. I got one last breath of air and then I was forced down again beneath the waves – the sail had me trapped!

Go down! I told myself. Swim down. And so I kicked out towards the sea floor until at last I felt free of the sail and then I swam upwards once more.

At the point when I truly thought I couldn't hold my breath a moment longer I broke the surface, coughing and sputtering as I took in the glorious air!

And then I swam as hard as I could away from the caravel. I saw the sea swallow it up like a hungry shark devouring a fish, gulping it down. The deck disappeared and then the water seemed to boil and the mast was suctioned down too. There was nothing left.

I could make out the black shapes of the horses dotting the waves ahead of me, swimming hard for the shore.

I fought the waves as hard as I could and tried to swim too, but I was weak. My legs had no strength left and my feeble kicks were not taking me any closer to shore. I was struggling to stay above the waves as they pummelled me, pushing me under again and again. The shore was not far from me, but it might as well have been as far away as Spain.

I have heard that drowning is the best death; that you simply give yourself over to the quietness of the water and sink to nothingness.

I can tell you this is not true. I fought my death with every last fibre of my being. As the water filled my lungs, I kicked and struggled and did everything I could, but when a huge wave drove me under and held me there I knew in my heart that I would not be able to fight my way to the surface again. As I sank down, I opened my eyes, to look upon the dark sea that consumed me. All I could see was black water. And then something else. A white apparition coming towards me.

Cara! I could see her underbelly and her legs, thrashing their way through the inky sea. She was churning her way through the waves, away from the other horses and the shore, coming towards me.

Coming for me.

At the sight of her, I fought once more. I began to kick as hard as I could, struggling back up to the surface, my arms pulling for all they were worth.

I broke through the waves, lungs aching, gasping for air. Cara saw me and swam nearer still.

"I'm here!" I cried out. The sea kept pushing her back, but then a sudden wave swept me towards her. I grasped hold of her mane with my trembling hands. Cara snorted and blew as she trod water and I clambered onboard her back.

I was so very weak I thought I might lose my grip and slip off, so I bound my hands tight in the coarse rope of her mane.

We had been in the water for what seemed like forever and yet the shore never seemed to grow closer. The ocean was brutal and it kept pushing against us, but beneath me, Cara struggled on valiantly. Her noble head was raised up high as she crested wave after wave, fighting her way to the dark land that lay ahead.

I knew we had reached the shore at last when the waves turned to white foam all around us. Cara gave vigorous snorts as she dug deep into the sand with her hooves, driving forward through the surf until we were free of the sea.

I was so cold by then, I had lost all feeling in my limbs. My fingers were blue and I struggled to untangle my hands from her mane. I got them free and then lost my balance and fell to the sand. It was dry and warm and I lay there, retching seawater from my lungs and gasping in air, unable to believe that I was alive. I was too weak to move, and I let myself give in to exhaustion. The last thing I saw as I closed my eyes was Cara, shining white in the moonlight, standing watch over me.

My protector, my saviour, my friend.

# Chosen

Five hundred years ago a Spanish caravel crashed into a reef trying to make an emergency landing in a storm. The ship was sunk but its captain, a young girl, made it to shore, along with seven horses – two stallions and five mares. One of them was a mare with a white face, strange markings and blue eyes. Her name was Cara Blanca.

Cara Blanca became queen of the herd on this tiny island and for centuries her blood survived from generation to generation. Now her sole remaining ancestor was out there on the Bonefish Marshes and about to be struck by a tropical storm that would devastate everything in its path.

Annie was right – the Duchess was special. She

224

was the last of the Medicine Hats. A living, breathing piece of history. And my fate was bound to her by a power that I didn't understand, yet felt more fiercely than the wind that stung at my cheeks, or the rain that soaked my skin.

It was impossible to see where I was going and I kept stumbling as I moved forward. The wind was so strong that the gusts repeatedly knocked me off my feet. I was down on my hands and knees, scrambling to get back up again when I heard the hoofbeats.

The Duchess was coming across the marshes with the herd right behind her. They were moving in frenzied, relentless gallop, flinging up sheets of muddy water in their wake.

I looked around for Annie and the tractor, thinking that they must be behind the horses.

"Annie!" I screamed out, but my voice was lost in the wind. "Annie! Where are you?"

But there was no Annie. It was just me.

I began to run across the marshes towards the horses, my arms waving, hoping to slow them down.

At the front of the herd, the Duchess looked like a mythical sea creature, her white legs pounding through the water, her pure white face looking otherworldly against the black stormy skies.

"Duchess!" I didn't know if she could even see me through the rain – she wasn't slowing down. I could see the herd behind her and I was right in their path.

The tremor of the hoofbeats shook the ground as the skies rumbled with thunder. I stood firm and called to her once more.

"Duchess!"

Suddenly, at the sound of my voice I saw a flicker in her pale blue eyes. She fixed me with her imperious gaze. Then she gave an anxious shake of her mane and deliberately slowed her strides. The rest of the herd began to scatter. They galloped off, veering left and right, leaping over tussock, stumbling in the seawater pools, while the Duchess kept coming right towards me.

She was only a few metres away, so close I could have almost touched her, when she jerked back and came to a sudden halt.

She stood there, flanks heaving, her nostrils flared so wide that I could see the pink skin inside them as her breath came in great shudders. She was exhausted, a froth of white sweat coating her chest and neck.

I was so relieved that she was safe. I wanted so

badly to throw my arms round her. But I was worried that if I moved too fast she would run again. And so I stood perfectly still, transfixed by her startling blue eyes.

And then, in front of me, the Duchess fell to her knees.

She dropped to the ground so quickly, I thought she had collapsed with exhaustion.

"Duchess!" I ran to her and by the time I reached her she was still down with her front legs bent beneath her. "Duchess, what's wrong?"

I was about to try and help her up when she snorted and put one of her legs out in front of her and then shook her magnificent mane and lowered her head so that her muzzle almost touched the ground.

She held the pose and then I realised. She was taking a bow.

It was so beautiful. I knew at that moment that what I was witnessing was ancient and deeply sacred.

The storm had been raging around us. Now, the rain stopped and the wind ceased and the sea didn't crash or roar. Everything in the world around me went still and all that was left was my horse and me.

The Duchess raised her head and she looked right at me, those blue eyes meeting my own. She stayed on one knee and I recalled Annie's words.

*Ain't nobody can ride a Medicine Hat – unless dey is chosen.*

I stepped forward and dropped into a curtsey, returning her bow. Then I moved closer to her shoulder and I reached out and touched her. My hands clutched her mane, fingers tangled into the strands. I was so cold that the warmth of her coat felt tingly against my frozen skin. I pressed hard against her, my heart slamming in my chest. I knew what I had to do, but I was scared to move. I know I am going to be a Grand Prix showjumper one day, but I had never been on a horse before in my life.

And then I jumped. I threw myself off the ground with all my strength, swinging my right leg up high and over the mare's rump, and at the same time with my arms I gripped the mane and pulled.

The Duchess felt the weight on her back as soon as I landed. She righted herself, getting up from her knees and as she did this I felt the ground rushing away from me.

And there I was, on the back of a wild horse.

I had no reins and no saddle and I was in the

path of an oncoming storm. The Duchess was facing directly across the Bonefish Marshes back towards the jungle where the track led to Annie's crib. We could make it before the storm hit and be safe.

"No," I whispered to the mare as she stepped forward. "We're not going that way. Not yet."

Out here on the marshes, even with Annie's help, I could never have saved the herd on foot. But now I was riding the Duchess. She was *de Boss Lady*.

"Come on, Duchess," I said. "We're going back for them."

The herd had scattered at the sight of me, but horses do not like to be separated for long and already they had begun to reform in a tight group. They had gathered not far from us, tense and alert, their senses heightened by the thunderstorm. One wrong move and they would scatter again. We had one chance – we had to do this right.

I willed the Duchess on, and she cantered in a wide loop round the rear of the herd. As we swept past, the Duchess slowed down and gave a loud whinny. The bay stallion immediately returned her call. Then he broke into a canter to follow her, and at his cue the others fell into formation right behind him.

I clung on tightly as we cantered back across the marshes. I could hear the thunder of their hoofbeats behind me, although I didn't dare look back. I was having enough trouble hanging on without looking over my shoulder. I had to trust that the Duchess's power was enough to hold them all the way home to Annie's.

I glanced over my shoulder just once and I was shocked to see the waves rising up at least three metres high, their white peaks crashing over the Bonefish Marshes, the trees bent so far over by the winds that their branches touched the ground.

The storm was surging at our heels. Up ahead, the jungle track was a tangle of branches, but there was no time to slow down. I crouched low over the Duchess's neck as she galloped on. I kept my eyes down and saw the ground rushing beneath her hooves. Behind us I could still hear the thunder of the herd. I twisted my fists even tighter into the Duchess's mane and buried my face against her neck.

As the path widened I lifted my head a little and heard hoofbeats coming up alongside us. The bay stallion was running right next to the Duchess.

He tried to barge past, fighting with every stride

to take the lead, and as his shoulders reached the Duchess's flanks he rammed us sideways. I gave a shriek as the Duchess lurched over. My legs slid, but my hands were tangled so tightly in her mane that I stayed onboard. I could feel the Duchess moving swiftly back underneath me so that I wouldn't fall. She waited until I had regained my balance and then with an arrogant snort and a sudden burst of speed, she surged forward. In just three strides she had taken the lead back from the bay stallion, reclaiming her rightful place at the head of the herd.

I knew we'd made it when I heard the sound of the bottle tree. The mad chorus of tinkling glass was chiming louder than cathedral bells above the howl of the gale.

We came in like a storm tide, a single mass of wild horses scattering around Annie, who stood there fearlessly in front of them.

"Bee-a-trizz! Dis way!"

The Duchess rode down the side of the cottage and the herd followed us straight into the pens without question. All of them except two stragglers at the back – mares who were so wild with fear, they kept spinning around at the sight of the gates.

"Yah! Yah!" Annie was jumping up and down

and waving her arms around, trying to get them to move forward, so she could get the gates shut.

"I'll come and help you!" I called out.

"No!" Annie shouted back. "Too dangerous! You get trampled!"

The other horses were getting agitated. The bay stallion broke loose from the herd and ran outside the gates. Annie blocked his path and tried to drive him back in again. We were losing them!

"I'm coming to help!"

"Stay there, Bee-a-trizz!" Annie shouted. "We got dis!"

And then I heard the engine revving and round the corner of the cottage Annie's big old tractor came rumbling into view. And sitting at the wheel, crunching the gears, was my mom.

She handled the tractor like a pro, parking it sideways across the gap between the cottage and the trees.

The horses were trapped – their only choice was to move forward and into the pens.

"Yah! Yah! C'mon!" Annie shouted.

"Yah Yah!" Mom jumped off the tractor and joined Annie, and the three loose horses knew they were beaten. They circled anxiously once more, and then they gave in and ran inside the shelter pen, barging alongside the others. Annie dashed straight up behind them, banging the gate closed and slipping the bolt hard across into its hole.

The Duchess gently stepped forward so that I could reach the high railing of the pen and I climbed off her back, vaulting over the rail. Then I leant my face up against the pen to look at her. She was exhausted from the gallop, heaving and blowing, but she was safe.

"Beatriz…"

And there was Mom by my side. She was all choked with emotion and she only managed to say my name, but that single word was filled with so much love and anger and joy that I started to cry, and so did she. She grabbed me so tight, I thought I wouldn't be able to keep breathing. "Oh, thank God! Bee!"

"Storm's almost here!" Annie was calling to us. "Come inside now!"

In the cottage we stood dripping and shivering on the rug while Annie dug out some yard clothes for us. "Get dressed," Annie said. "Get yo' selve under the blankets and I gonna make us all a hot brew o' tea."

For the next few hours the whole cottage shook

so much I truly believed we were going to be lifted up off the ground. Mom and I spent most of that time huddled on the sofa, listening to every screech and crack. Annie kept on pottering about the place, unable to stay still. She was humming away and if I hadn't known better I would have thought she was enjoying herself. But I knew Annie hummed like this when she was anxious, to hide the nerves that knotted in her belly.

"Will the horses be all right out there?" I asked.

"Sure dey will," Annie said softly. "You did good, Beatriz. You did real good, getting them home."

I looked over at Mom, expecting to see her looking angry. But she had tears in her eyes.

"Beatriz," she said. "I'm sorry I never listened. About the horses."

"It's OK," I said.

"And I'm sorry about your dad. I should never have told you. Not like that…"

"No," I shook my head. "I knew what he was, but I pretended, you know? I guess I have to stop pretending now."

I looked out through the storm shutters. The wind was still howling. The rain was coming down in sheets.

"Will the *Phaedra* be all right in this?" I asked.

234

Mom smiled ruefully. "No, probably not. The weather was cutting up pretty rough in the bay when I left. I drove her as close to the shore as I could get and then waded in from there. I managed to get her anchored, but the waves were big and she's a tiny boat. I don't know how she'll hold up when the hurricane peaks."

"What about all your work stuff?"

Mom looked wistful. "It's all back on the *Phaedra*."

Mom pulled me closer and put her arm round me.

"It'll be OK, Beatriz," Mom said. "Everything that matters to me is right here."

And we sat there in silence, the three of us, and listened to the storm and drank our gumbo-limbo tea.

# After the Storm

My name is Beatriz Ortega and this will be my last diary entry...

We all survived that night – Me, Mom, Annie and the horses. The weather reports afterwards called the storm a force nine gale – the worst hurricane to ever hit Great Abaco island.

At Marsh Harbour, the windows were smashed all the way down the main street and the dive shop had its roof taken clean off.

The whole second floor of Wally's got destroyed when a massive palm tree fell on it. Luckily no one was hurt. Oh, and the kiosk down at the marina isn't there any more. It was totally flattened.

The coastal areas, like the Bonefish Marshes, were

devastated. The hurricane tore apart everything in its path. Sand dunes were disintegrated. Trees were uprooted and flung about like matchsticks.

Mom always says that even though I was wrong to disobey her that day, I did the right thing. She's glad I saved the horses and she's never blamed me for what happened to the *Phaedra*.

The storm must have swept the *Phaedra* off her anchor. Mom thinks she probably struck the reef and got broken up and sank. I think of her sometimes, my old home, submerged in the bay alongside Felipa Molina's lost caravel.

When the *Phaedra* went down Mom lost all her jellyfish equipment, but she'd pocketed her flash drive and managed to finish the research paper she'd been working on. When the university published her jellyfish report a few months later it was big news in marine biology circles. Mom got loads of job offers. Most of them involved going out and living at sea again, but the one Mom accepted took us home, back to Florida, which is where we live now.

I've been settling into life here, although it feels a little strange at times to be on dry land and stay in one place.

My first day at high school, I was pretty scared. I mean, hello, home-schooler for three years and suddenly I'm in a school with six hundred other kids? But guess who was in my class on the first day? Kristen Adams. Annie was right about her too, because she's been a really good friend ever since I got back. We laugh about how we used to play horses together and sometimes she comes with me when I have riding lessons.

I go every week to the local stables – sometimes twice a week. Mom says maybe now we're back and all settled in she might even buy me a horse. *Buy me a horse.* That sounds weird, right? I mean, I never *bought* the Duchess. She had simply been mine from the moment we met. She was wild, but she belonged to me – and I belonged to her too. And even now, she still owns my heart in the way no other horse ever will.

When we left Great Abaco I tried to convince Annie to start using email. But Annie is stubborn.

"Mercy no, Bee-a-trizz," she told me. "There's too much talkin' in de world already. If you really got sometink to say, pick up de pen an' paper an' write it to me."

So I sent Annie letters telling her about me and

school and the stables and life in Florida, but I didn't hear anything back. Months went by, almost a year maybe. Then in February, just as the spring weather was turning warm, I got a letter with a postmark from the Bahamas. It wasn't much longer than an email. Or even a tweet.

*The Duchess is having herself a foal.* Annie wrote. *Due any day now. Come back to the island – you need to be here.*

This time we didn't sail into Great Abaco – we flew in on a five-seater Cessna. Mom came with me. She and Annie had got quite close after the storm. And I think she wanted to see the Duchess's foal every bit as much as I did.

We hired bicycles at the hotel. There wasn't much use in taking a car if you were trying to get to Annie's. As we rode through the rutted dirt tracks into the jungle I felt the weight of the books in my backpack thumping up and down against my spine.

"Bee-a-trizz!" Annie was on the porch waiting to greet us. I guess the good thing about being an old person is that you never really look much older, because Annie looked exactly the same as the last time I had seen her.

"I got a girl who been a dyin' fa to meet you," she smiled. "Come with me."

Annie got on the tractor and beckoned me to take my old position sitting up on her wheel arch.

"Are you coming?" I asked Mom.

"No." She shook her head. "Not just yet. You two go on ahead."

And so we set off, me and Annie, just like that first day when she found me and pulled me out of the mud hole, heading off through the jungle.

We found the Duchess and her filly out by the Bonefish Marshes. They were grazing together right at the very edge of the herd. The filly kept straying off and I watched the Duchess follow after her, acting real casual so that the filly never noticed, always guiding her back towards the safety of the herd.

"She's a good mama," Annie confirmed. "She's raising that filly just right."

At the sight of the tractor the Duchess didn't raise the alarm to the herd. She simply lowered her neck back down to graze. Then I called out to her, and suddenly she raised her head and looked at us, her ears pricked.

"Look! She still know you, Bee-a-trizz!" Annie smiled. "She still know you."

The Duchess broke into a trot towards us, the filly keeping pace alongside her, looking wide-eyed. I had to laugh at the way the little filly held her head aloft. She had that same proud look as her mom. All high and mighty, like she knew that she was descended from royalty.

And she was like a mirror image of her mother too – a Medicine Hat with perfect markings, the brown bonnet over the ears and the splash of colour on her rump and a shield at her chest.

When they reached us, the Duchess stood a little way back and Annie gestured for me to step forward on my own. I took a few steps, nervous at first, and then I couldn't help it. I ran the rest of the way and threw my arms round her neck, hugging her tight.

"Hey, Duchess." I breathed in her warm scent. "Did you miss me?"

The Duchess nuzzled at my hair, her velvet muzzle tickling my neck. I let her go and turned my attention to her foal, who was sniffing inquisitively at the hem of my shirt.

"Hello, little one." I reached out to stroke her white face. "Nice to meet you. I'm an old friend of your mama's."

We stayed at Annie's place that night. She and Mom must have drunk a gallon of tea as they stayed up and talked. We ate okra and shrimp gumbo for dinner and Mom and I slept on the sofa under Annie's soft blue blanket.

I woke up a little before dawn and dressed as quietly as I could so as not to wake Mom and Annie. On the porch I pulled on my shoes and then I dug through my backpack to make sure I had both of the diaries packed in there.

Felipa's diary was even more weathered now after everything it had been through. The pages were well thumbed too. I must have read the whole thing at least a dozen times. The final pages that Felipa wrote after the shipwreck were the ones I reread the most and I knew the words off by heart.

After the storm had passed, Felipa had salvaged as much as she could from the wreckage of the caravel. Some of the cargo had washed up on the shore. Other pieces she managed to retrieve by swimming out into the bay and dragging them back to the beach. One of the things she rescued from the waves was the ship's chest, containing the last of her personal possessions – her diary and her velvet gown.

I can no longer write the date on my entries, Felipa writes...

For I no longer know what day it is. I have ridden Cara all over the island and I am satisfied that it is quite deserted. So I have no one to speak to. This diary is my only conversation and the horses my only companions.

I am not lonely. When I had friends they disappointed me, and when I lived with men they revolted me. All except Juan – but I must accept that he is lost to me forever. If I am to spend the rest of my days here with the herd and my beloved Cara, I shall be quite happy.

In my travels around the island I have found the perfect place for us. There is a tree in a pretty clearing with broad branches that is the ideal place to make camp. I have built myself a thatched roof by entwining palm leaves in the branches and making walls and a floor from the leaves. The days are hot here but the nights are not cold and it is enough to shelter me. Sometimes Cara will come inside my thatched hut at night and we sleep together, curled up on the floor. It reminds me of being in the stables together at the Alhambra.

But here there are no fences like there were in Spain. The mares and stallions roam the island and eat the marsh grasses and the vines. Cara is their leader, of course. She still allows me to ride her and sometimes I will fling myself on her back and go galloping down the beach just for the sheer joy of feeling the wind in my face and the speed of her powerful strides beneath me.

I think of Spain at those moments too. I remember the ride on the road to Cadiz to catch Admiral Columbus with the message from the Queen. Cara was the fastest horse in the Queen's stables. She was groomed and fed and braided and dressed in the finest livery. Now she lives rough and unfettered with the sun bleaching her coat and the tussock knotting her mane like a ragamuffin. All the same, there is still a sense of nobility about her. She knows she is special.

I have noticed for a while that Cara's belly is swelling. I thought at first that she was getting fat on the marsh grass, but now I realise she is pregnant. Soon she will have her first foal. I hope it will bear the same markings as Cara — the white face and the shield on her chest — the mark of the protector...

The final diary entry from Felipa appears just a few pages later. These are the last words she writes:

I saw a boat yesterday. I sat on the beach and watched the sails in the distance, and after a long while I could see that it was coming closer.

I considered what to do and decided that I would not run and hide.

I went back to my shelter at the tree and from the ship's chest I pulled out my old velvet gown. It had been such a long while since I had worn it. How queer it felt to fasten tight the corset against my chest! It took me forever to thread the ribbons.

Once I was dressed I undid my braids and let my long dark hair fall loose over my shoulders. For wasn't I the queen of my own land now? Did I not deserve to be dressed as such?

And so I watched and I waited as the boat anchored in the cove. I could only see one sailor aboard the vessel and I watched with intrigue as he lowered a rowing boat over the side and made for the shore. His face was shaded by one of those wide-brimmed hats that the boatswain had worn on our voyage from Spain, and as he came towards me I knew there was something very familiar about him. I thought I must be imagining it, but as the boat drew to shore and I could see his face at last, I knew it to be true. It was Juan!

I ran down the beach to meet him and even before I was in his arms I was sobbing. "You found me!" I kept saying over and over again. "How did you ever find me?"

"Because I never gave up looking," Juan said. And he told me the whole story, about almost being captured by the sailors when he went to take the stallions that night, how he had hidden and waited for them to move on, but as he did so, someone must have noticed that the other horses were gone and raised the alarm. He saw the mob of sailors armed with torches and realised he could not get back to the jetty without being captured.

"When I heard that you had got away it gave me hope," Juan said. "I had to believe that you were out there somewhere and I never gave up hope that you were alive. So I combed the oceans to find you."

The search had taken him almost a year, across countless islands from Hispaniola to here.

"When I left Spain I wanted to see the world – and I've seen so much, Felipa," he said. "Now I plan to return, to go home, and I want you to come with me."

"You mean Spain? But I cannot leave! Cara is about to foal – and we could not carry enough food on your ship for the horses. They would never survive the journey."

Juan shook his head. "I don't mean the horses, Felipa. They are wild now. They have made their home here. I mean you. Just you and me."

"But…" I began to speak, but before I could continue Juan had dropped to one knee and clasped my hand in his own.

"Felipa," Juan said, "from the moment I met you I have known that I would be unable to live without you. I have risked my life for you and sailed the oceans to find you. There is no life for us here. I am on bended knee asking you to marry me. Come away with me and return to Spain!"

I did not know what to do. I knew in my heart that I loved Juan. But to say farewell to Cara?

"I need to think," I said.

Juan's face fell.

"I understand," he replied. "But when dawn breaks, I will be leaving. If you love me too then you will come with me."

I hardly slept that night. When I did, my dreams were feverish – I was drowning and I could see Cara coming for me, lifting me up on her back above the waves and taking me to safety. But this time when we emerged from the surf and I lay gasping on the sand she raised her head up to the breeze and then she galloped on without me.

And then I opened my eyes and saw Juan was lying beside me. I shook him gently by the shoulder.

"Wake up," I said. "I have made up my mind."

I will not describe how much it breaks my heart as I write these final words. I have decided to go with Juan and I know it is the right thing to do, but it means saying goodbye to my beloved Cara. After all we have been through together, it is like leaving a piece of my soul behind.

Juan says that in Spain we shall start a new chapter in our lives. And so it seems fitting to leave this, my old life, behind. I have carved a hole in the trunk of the tree that I have made my home for all these months. It is large enough to serve as a treasure trove for my diary. For in truth, it is not my diary to keep. It is the story of Cara and it should stay here with her, just as a piece of my heart will forever. She is my Cara Blanca, my dearest, and I will love her always…

*If you're going to give the diary back, you should give it to the tree.* That was what Annie said to me once. And so there I was back on Great Abaco, and I knew that the time had come for me to return Felipa's diary to the place it came from.

As I walked through the jungle and saw the sun rise through the canopy of the trees above me, I felt a certainty, just as Felipa did when she wrapped her diary in her old sailor shirt over five hundred years ago and nestled it inside the Jumbie tree.

The hole that Felipa carved into the trunk is much higher up now than it was way back then and I had to climb up to reach it. I carefully pushed Felipa's diary in as deep as it would go. Then I pulled my own diary out of my backpack, wrapping it in an old T-shirt before I placed it inside the tree.

Felipa's diary and mine, side by side. They sit there and wait. Ready for the next guardians of the Medicine Hat to find.

It was fate that brought me here to tell my story.

And now fate has given the power of the obeah to the next generation. If you are reading this book, then it means that my diary is in good hands.

Be the guardian of the words, just as I was.

My horses belong to you now.

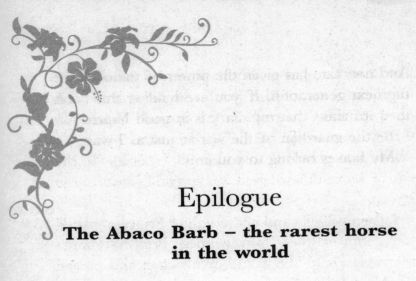

# Epilogue

## The Abaco Barb – the rarest horse in the world

How did a wild herd of Spanish horses wind up on a small island in the Bahamas?

No one is certain, but the most convincing theory is that a small herd of Spanish horses travelled with Christopher Columbus on his second voyage, surviving a shipwreck to establish a herd on Great Abaco Island.

DNA tests have proven that the horses on Great Abaco have incredibly pure bloodlines that can be traced directly to fifteenth-century Spain.

Many of the historical facts in this novel are true. The real Queen Isabella did change her mind and send a rider after Columbus to give him the good news on the road to Cadiz. She also ordered the mass expulsion of the Jews, and the torture and death of the Conversos in the Spanish Inquisition that was led by Tomas de Torquemada. The black plague was greatly feared in 1493, especially in the city of Barcelona where it was spread by fleas borne on rats.

Queen Isabella and her daughter Princess Joanna were both excellent horsewomen. Princess Joanna married 'Philip the Handsome' when she turned sixteen, but the marriage was an unhappy one and she became deeply tormented. After Philip died Joanna was confined to a nunnery and is known in the history books as 'Joanna the Mad'.

Today it is very rare to find a true black horse in Spain and the legend says this is because Queen Isabella considered black horses to be possessed by the devil and ruled that black horses must be killed at birth.

The blue eyes and shield and bonnet markings of Cara and the Duchess can still be seen on modern-day horses in both Spain and in the Americas. The term 'Medicine Hat' was given to these horses by the Native Americans. It is their belief that these horses possess powerful magic. They

say a Medicine Hat horse will choose their rider
and keep them safe from harm: a protector, and the
truest of friends.